Leveled Texts
for
Classic Fiction

Humor

Collected and Leveled by Stephanie Paris

SHELL EDUCATION

Contributing Author

Wendy Conklin, M.S.

Publishing Credits

Dona Herweck Rice, *Editor-in-Chief*; Robin Erickson, *Production Director*; Lee Aucoin, *Creative Director*; Timothy J. Bradley, *Illustration Manager*; Sara Johnson, M.S.Ed., *Senior Editor*; Evelyn Garcia, *Associate Education Editor*; Grace Alba, *Designer*; Corinne Burton, M.A.Ed., *Publisher*

Image Credits

All images Shutterstock

Standards
© 2004 Mid-continent Research for Education and Learning (McREL)
© 2010 National Governors Association Center for Best Practices and Council of Chief State School Officers (CCSS)

Shell Education

5301 Oceanus Drive
Huntington Beach, CA 92649
http://www.shelleducation.com
ISBN 978-1-4258-0988-1

© 2013 Shell Educational Publishing, Inc.

Table of Contents

What Is Fiction?

Fiction is the work of imaginative narration. In other words, it is something that is made, as opposed to something that has happened or something that is discovered. It helps bring our imaginations to life, since it offers an escape into a world where everything happens for a reason—nothing is by chance. Fiction includes three main elements: plot (sequence), character, and setting (place).

Each event occurs in a logical order, and somehow, the conflict is resolved. Fiction promises a resolution in the end, and so the reader waits for resolution as the characters change, grow, and survive experiences. We are drawn to fiction because it is very close to the story of our lives. Fiction suggests that our own stories will have meaning and a resolution in the end. Perhaps that might be the reason why we love fiction—it delivers what it promises.

Fiction compels its readers to care about the characters whether they are loyal friends or conniving enemies. Readers dream about the characters and mourn their heartaches. Readers might feel that they know a fictional character's story intimately because he or she reminds them of a friend or family member. Additionally, the place described in the story might feel like a real place the reader has visited or would like to visit.

Fiction vs. Nonfiction

Fiction is literature that stems from the imagination and includes genres such as mystery, adventure, fairy tales, and fantasy. Fiction can include facts, but the story is not true in its entirety. Facts are often exaggerated or manipulated to suit an author's intent for the story. Realistic fiction uses plausible characters and storylines, but the people do not really exist and/or the events narrated did not ever really take place. In addition, fiction is descriptive, elaborate, and designed to entertain. It allows readers to make their own interpretations based on the text.

Nonfiction includes a wide variety of writing styles that deal exclusively with real events, people, places, and things such as biographies, cookbooks, historical records, and scientific reports. Nonfiction is literature based on facts or perceived facts. In literature form, nonfiction deals with events that have actually taken place and relies on existing facts. Nonfiction writing is entirely fact-based. It states only enough to establish a fact or idea and is meant to be informative. Nonfiction is typically direct, clear, and simple in its message. Despite the differences, both fiction and nonfiction have a benefit and purpose for all readers.

The Importance of Using Fiction

Reading fiction has many benefits: It stimulates the imagination, promotes creative thinking, increases vocabulary, and improves writing skills. However, "students often hold negative attitudes about reading because of dull textbooks or being forced to read" (Bean 2000).

Fiction books can stimulate imagination. It is easy to get carried away with the character Percy Jackson as he battles the gods in *The Lightning Thief* (Riordan 2005). Readers can visualize what the author depicts. Researcher Keith Oatley (2009) states that fiction allows individuals to stimulate the minds of others in a sense of expanding on how characters might be feeling and what they might be thinking. When one reads fiction, one cannot help but visualize the nonexistent characters and places of the story. Lisa Zunshine (2006) has emphasized that fiction allows readers to engage in a theory-of-mind ability that helps them practice what the characters experience.

Since the work of fiction is indirect, it requires analysis if one is to get beyond the surface of the story. On the surface, one can view *Moby Dick* (Melville 1851) as an adventure story about a man hunting a whale. On closer examination and interpretation, the novel might be seen as a portrayal of good and evil. When a reader examines, interprets, and analyzes a work of fiction, he or she is promoting creative thinking. Creativity is a priceless commodity, as it facilitates problem solving, inventions, and creations of all kinds, and promotes personal satisfaction as well.

Reading fiction also helps readers build their vocabularies. Readers cannot help but learn a myriad of new words in Lemony Snicket's *A Series of Unfortunate Events* (1999). Word knowledge and reading comprehension go hand in hand. In fact, "vocabulary knowledge is one of the best predictors of reading achievement" (Richek 2005). Further, "vocabulary knowledge promotes reading fluency, boosts reading comprehension, improves academic achievement, and enhances thinking and communication" (Bromley 2004). Most researchers believe that students have the ability to add between 2,000 to 3,000 new words each school year, and by fifth grade, that number can be as high as 10,000 new words in their reading alone (Nagy and Anderson 1984). By exposing students to a variety of reading selections, educators can encourage students to promote the vocabulary growth that they need to be successful.

Finally, reading fictional text has a strong impact on students' ability as writers. According to Gay Su Pinnell (1988), "As children read and write, they make the connections that form their basic understandings about both….There is ample evidence to suggest that the processes are inseparable and that teachers should examine pedagogy in the light of these interrelationships." Many of the elements students encounter while reading fiction can transition into their writing abilities.

The Importance of Using Fiction (cont.)

Text Complexity

Text complexity refers to reading and comprehending various texts with increasing complexity as students progress through school and within their reading development. The Common Core State Standards (2010) state that "by the time they [students] complete the core, students must be able to read and comprehend independently and proficiently the kinds of complex texts commonly found in college and careers." In other words, by the time students complete high school, they must be able to read and comprehend highly complex texts, so students must consistently increase the level of complexity tackled at each grade level. Text complexity relies on the following combination of quantitative and qualitative factors:

Quantitative Factors	
Word Frequency	This is how often a particular word appears in the text. If an unfamiliar high-frequency word appears in a text, chances are the student will have a difficult time understanding the meaning of the text.
Sentence Length	Long sentences and sentences with embedded clauses require a lot from a young reader.
Word Length	This is the number of syllables in a word. Longer words are not by definition hard to read, but certainly can be for young readers.
Text Length	This refers to the number of words within the text passage.
Text Cohesion	This is the overall structure of the text. A high-cohesion text guides readers by signaling relationships among sentences through repetition and concrete language. A low-cohesion text does not have such support.

The Importance of Using Fiction (cont.)

Qualitative Factors	
Level of Meaning or Purpose of Text	This refers to the objective and/or purpose for reading.
Structure	Texts that display low complexity are known for their simple structure. Texts that display high complexity are known for disruptions to predictable understandings.
Language Convention and Clarity	Texts that deviate from contemporary use of English tend to be more challenging to interpret.
Knowledge Demands	This refers to the background knowledge students are expected to have prior to reading a text. Texts that require students to possess a certain amount of previous knowledge are more complex than those that assume students have no prior knowledge.

(Adapted from the National Governors Association Center for Best Practices and Council of Chief State School Officers 2010)

The use of qualitative and quantitative measures to assess text complexity is demonstrated in the expectation that educators possess the ability to match the appropriate texts to the appropriate students. The passages in *Leveled Texts for Classic Fiction: Humor* vary in text complexity and will provide leveled versions of classic complex texts so that educators can scaffold students' comprehension of these texts. Educators can choose passages for students to read based on the reading level as well as the qualitative and quantitative complexity factors in order to find texts that are "just right" instructionally.

Genres of Fiction

There are many different fiction genres. The *Leveled Texts for Classic Fiction* series focuses on the following genres: adventure, fantasy and science fiction, mystery, historical fiction, mythology, humor, and Shakespeare.

Adventure stories transport readers to exotic places like deserted islands, treacherous mountains, and the high seas. This genre is dominated by fast-paced action. The plot often focuses on a hero's quest and features a posse that helps him or her achieve the goal. The story confronts the protagonist with events that disrupt his or her normal life and puts the character in danger. The story involves exploring and conquering the unknown accompanied by much physical action, excitement, and risk. The experience changes the protagonist in many ways.

The Importance of Using Fiction (cont.)

Fantasy and science fiction are closely related. Fantasy, like adventure, involves quests or journeys that the hero must undertake. Within fantasy, magic and the supernatural are central and are used to suggest universal truths. Events happen outside the laws that govern our universe. Science fiction also operates outside of the laws of physics but typically takes place in the future, space, another world, or an alternate dimension. Technology plays a strong role in this genre. Both science fiction and fantasy open up possibilities (such as living in outer space and talking to animals) because the boundaries of the real world cannot confine the story. Ideas are often expressed using symbols.

Mystery contains intriguing characters with suspenseful plots and can often feel very realistic. The story revolves around a problem or puzzle to solve: *Who did it? What is it? How did it happen?* Something is unknown, or a crime needs to be solved. Authors give readers clues to the solution in a mystery, but they also distract the reader by intentionally misleading them.

Historical fiction focuses on a time period from the past with the intent of offering insight into what it was like to live during that time. This genre incorporates historical research into the stories to make them feel believable. However, much of the story is fictionalized, whether it is conversations or characters. Often, these stories reveal that concerns from the past are still concerns. Historical fiction centers on historical events, periods, or figures.

Myths are collections of sacred stories from ancient societies. Myths are ways to explain questions about the creation of the world, the gods, and human life. For example, mythological stories often explain why natural events like storms or floods occur or how the world and living things came to be in existence. Myths can be filled with adventures conflict, between humans, and gods with extraordinary powers. These gods possess emotions and personality traits that are similar to humans.

Humor can include parody, joke books, spoofs, and twisted tales, among others. Humorous stories are written with the intent of being light-hearted and fun in order to make people laugh and to entertain. Often, these stories are written with satire and dry wit. Humorous stories also can have a very serious or dark side, but the ways in which the characters react and handle the situations make them humorous.

Shakespeare's plays can be classified in three genres: comedy, tragedy, and history. Shakespeare wrote his plays during the late 1500s and early 1600s, and performed many of them in the famous Globe Theater in London, England. Within each play is not just one coherent story but also a set of two or three stories that can be described as "plays within a play." His plays offer multiple perspectives and contradictions to make the stories rich and interesting. Shakespeare is noted for his ability to bring thoughts to life. He used his imagination to adapt stories, history, and other plays to entertain his audiences.

Elements of Fiction

The many common characteristics found throughout fiction are known as the elements of fiction. Among such elements are *point of view*, *character*, *setting*, and *plot*. *Leveled Texts for Classic Fiction* concentrates on setting, plot, and character, with an emphasis on language usage.

Language usage typically refers to the rules for making language. This series includes the following elements: *personification*, *hyperbole*, *alliteration*, *onomatopoeia*, *imagery*, *symbolism*, *metaphor*, and *word choice*. The table below provides a brief description of each.

Language Usage	Definition	Example
Personification	Giving human traits to nonhuman things	The chair moaned when she sat down on it.
Hyperbole	Extreme exaggeration	He was so hungry, he could eat a horse.
Alliteration	Repetition of the beginning consonant sounds	She sold seashells by the seashore.
Onomatopoeia	Forming a word from the sound it makes	Knock-knock, woof, bang, sizzle, hiss
Imagery	Language that creates a meaningful visual experience for the reader	His socks filled the room with a smell similar to a wet dog on a hot day.
Symbolism	Using objects to represent something else	A heart represents *love*.
Metaphor	Comparison of two unrelated things	My father is the rock of our family.
Word Choice	Words that an author uses to make the story memorable and to capture the reader's attention	In chapter two of *Holes* by Louis Sachar (2000), the author directly addresses the reader, saying, "The reader is probably asking…." The author predicts what the reader is wondering.

Elements of Fiction *(cont.)*

Setting is the *where* and *when* of a story's action. Understanding setting is important to the interpretation of the story. The setting takes readers to other times and places. Setting plays a large part in what makes a story enjoyable for the reader.

Plot forms the core of what the story is about and establishes the chain of events that unfolds in the story. Plot contains a character's motivation and the subsequent cause and effect of the character's actions. A plot diagram is an organizational tool that focuses on mapping out the events in a story. By mapping out the plot structure, students are able to visualize the key features of a story. The following is an example of a plot diagram:

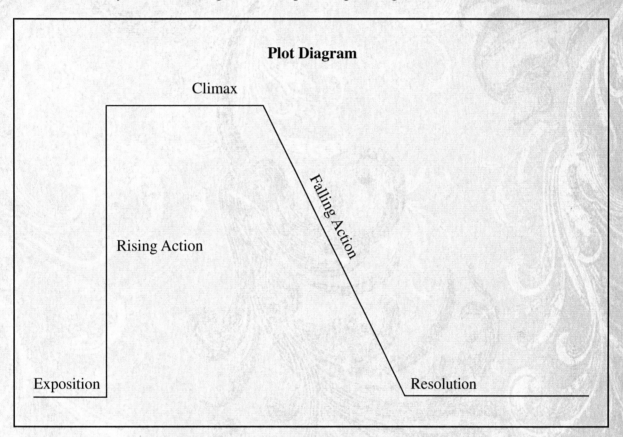

Plot Diagram

Climax

Falling Action

Rising Action

Exposition

Resolution

Characters are the people in the story. The protagonist is the main or leading character. He or she might be the narrator of the story. The antagonist is the force or character that acts against the protagonist. This antagonist is not always a person; it could be things such as weather, technology, or even a vehicle. Both the protagonist and antagonist can be considered dynamic, which means that they change or grow during the story as opposed to remaining static, or unchanging, characters. Readers engage with the text as they try to understand what motivates the characters to think and act as they do. Desires, values, and outside pressures all motivate characters' actions and help to determine the story's outcome.

A Closer Look at Humor

Humor stories are written with the intent of being light-hearted and funny. The author writes them for entertainment, but the stories are subjective to the reader's sense of humor. The humor can range from satire, dry wit, or dark humor, but it is the characters that handle any given situation who make it funny. Even very serious topics can be placed in this genre as long as the characters react in humorous fashions. Also, humor stories tend to have happy endings.

In this book, you will find stories from classic fiction works of humor. The titles are as follows:

- *The Adventures of Pinocchio* by C. Collodi
- *Mother Goose in Prose* by L. Frank Baum
- *Denslow's Three Bears* by W. W. Denslow
- *Alice's Adventures in Wonderland* by Lewis Carroll
- *Anne of Green Gables* by Lucy Maud Montgomery
- *The Magic Fishbone: A Holiday Romance from the Pen of Miss Alice Rainbird* by Charles Dickens
- *The Book of Nature Myths: Why the Bear Has a Short Tail* by Florence Holbrook
- *The Bremen Town Musicians* by The Brothers Grimm
- *Clever Else* by The Brothers Grimm
- *The Story of Doctor Dolittle* by Hugh Lofting
- *Tales from Shakespeare* by Charles and Mary Lamb
- *The Celebrated Jumping Frog of Calaveras County* by Mark Twain
- *How the Camel Got His Hump* by Rudyard Kippling
- *My Father's Dragon* by Ruth Stiles Gannett
- *The Wonderful Wizard of Oz* by L. Frank Baum

A Closer Look at Humor (cont.)

Although there are many elements of fiction that can be studied in each passage of this book, the chart below outlines the strongest element portrayed in each passage.

Element of Fiction	Passage Title
Setting	• Excerpt from *The Adventures of Pinocchio* • Excerpt from *Mother Goose in Prose* • Excerpt from *Denslow's Three Bears*
Character	• Excerpt from *Alice's Adventures in Wonderland* • Excerpt from *Anne of Green Gables* • Excerpt from *The Magic Fishbone: A Holiday Romance from the Pen of Miss Alice Rainbird* • Excerpt from *The Book of Nature Myths: Why the Bear Has a Short Tail*
Plot	• Excerpt from *The Bremen Town Musicians* • Excerpt from *Clever Else* • Excerpt from *The Story of Doctor Dolittle* • Excerpt from *Tales from Shakespeare*
Language Usage	• Excerpt from *The Celebrated Jumping Frog of Calaveras County* • Excerpt from *How the Camel Got His Hump* • Excerpt from *My Father's Dragon* • Excerpt from *The Wonderful Wizard of Oz*

Leveled Texts to Differentiate Instruction

Today's classrooms contain diverse pools of learners. Above-level, on-level, below-level, and English language learners all come together to learn from one teacher in one classroom. The teacher is expected to meet their diverse needs. These students have different learning styles, come from different cultures, experience a variety of emotions, and have varied interests. And, they differ in academic readiness when it comes to reading. At times, the challenges teachers face can be overwhelming as they struggle to create learning environments that address the differences in their students while at the same time ensure that all students master the required grade-level objectives.

What is differentiation? Tomlinson and Imbau say, "Differentiation is simply a teacher attending to the learning needs of a particular student or small group of students, rather than teaching a class as though all individuals in it were basically alike" (2010). Any teacher who keeps learners at the forefront of his or her instruction can successfully provide differentiation. The effective teacher asks, "What am I going to do to shape instruction to meet the needs of all my learners?" One method or methodology will not reach all students.

Differentiation includes what is taught, how it is taught, and the products students create to show what they have learned. When differentiating curriculum, teachers become organizers of learning opportunities within the classroom environment. These opportunities are often referred to as *content*, *process*, and *product*.

- **Content:** Differentiating the content means to put more depth into the curriculum through organizing the curriculum concepts and structure of knowledge.

- **Process:** Differentiating the process requires using varied instructional techniques and materials to enhance student learning.

- **Product:** Cognitive development and students' abilities to express themselves improves when products are differentiated.

Leveled Texts to Differentiate Instruction *(cont.)*

Teachers should differentiate by content, process, and product according to students' differences. These differences include student *readiness*, *learning styles*, and *interests*.

- **Readiness:** If a learning experience aligns closely with students' previous skills and understanding of a topic, they will learn better.

- **Learning styles:** Teachers should create assignments that allow students to complete work according to their personal preferences and styles.

- **Interests:** If a topic sparks excitement in the learners, then students will become involved in learning and better remember what is taught.

Typically, reading teachers select different novels or texts that are leveled for their classrooms because only one book may either be too difficult or too easy for a particular group of students. One group of students will read one novel while another group reads another, and so on. What makes *Leveled Texts for Classic Fiction: Humor* unique is that all students, regardless of reading level, can read the same selection from a story and can participate in whole-class discussions about it. This is possible because each selection is leveled at four different reading levels to accommodate students' reading abilities. Regardless of the reading level, all of the selections present the same content. Teachers can then focus on the same content standard or objective for the whole class, but individual students can access the content at their particular instructional levels rather than their frustration level and avoid the frustration of a selection at too high or low a level.

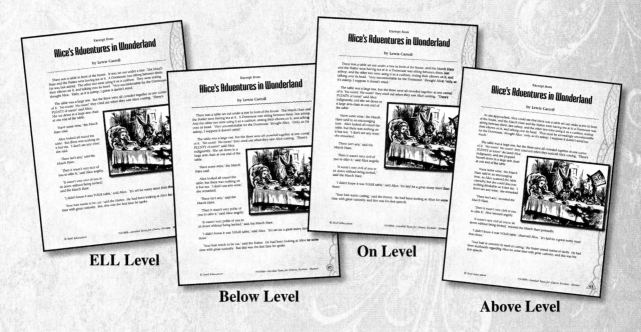

ELL Level

Below Level

On Level

Above Level

Leveled Texts to Differentiate Instruction *(cont.)*

Teachers should use the texts in this series to scaffold the content for their students. At the beginning of the year, students at the lowest reading levels may need focused teacher guidance. As the year progresses, teachers can begin giving students multiple levels of the same text to allow them to work independently at improving their comprehension. This means that each student will have a copy of the text at his or her independent reading level and at the instructional reading level. As students read the instructional-level texts, they can use the lower-leveled texts to better understand difficult vocabulary. By scaffolding the content in this way, teachers can support students as they move up through the reading levels and encourage them to work with texts that are closer to the grade level at which they will be tested.

A teacher does not need to draw attention to the fact that the texts are leveled. Nor should they hide it. Teachers who want students to read the text together can use homogeneous groups and distribute the texts after students join the groups. Or, teachers can distribute copies of the appropriate level to each student by copying the pages and separating them by each level.

Teaching Suggestions

Strategies for Higher-Order Thinking

Open-ended questions are a great way to infuse higher-order thinking skills into instruction. Open-ended questions have many appropriate answers and are exclusively dependent on the creativity of the student. Rarely do these questions have only one correct answer. It is up to the students to think and decide on their own what the answer should be. This is critical thinking at its very best. The following are some characteristics of open-ended questions:

- They ask students to *think* and *reflect*.
- They ask students to provide their *feelings* and *opinions*.
- They make students responsible for the *control* of the conversation.

There are many reasons to prefer open-ended over closed-ended questions. First, students must know the facts of the story to answer open-ended questions. Any higher-order question by necessity will encompass lower-order, fact-based questions. For a student to be able to answer a *what if* question (which is an example of an open-ended question), he or she must know the content of the story (which is a lower-level fact).

Open-ended questions also stimulate students to go beyond typical questions about a text. They spark real conversations about a text and are enriching. As a result, more students will be eager to participate in class discussions. In a more dynamic atmosphere, students will naturally make outside connections to the text, and there will be no need to force such connections.

Some students may at first be resistant to open-ended questions because they are afraid to think creatively. Years of looking for the one correct answer may make many students fear failure and embarrassment if they get the "wrong" answer. It will take time for these students to feel at ease with these questions. Model how to answer such questions. Keep encouraging students to answer them. Most importantly, be patient. The following are some examples of open-ended questions:

- Why do you think the author selected this setting?
- What are some explanations for the character's decisions?
- What are some lessons that this passage can teach us?
- How do the words set the mood or tone of this passage?

Teaching Suggestions *(cont.)*

Strategies for Higher-Order Thinking *(cont.)*

The tables below and on the following page are examples of open-ended questions and question stems that are specific to the elements of fiction covered in this series. Choose questions to challenge students to think more deeply about specific elements.

Setting
• In what ways did the setting…
• Describe the ways in which the author used setting to…
• What if the setting changed to…
• What are some possible explanations for selecting this setting?
• What would be a better setting for this story, and why is it better?
• Why did the author select this setting?
• What new element would you add to this setting to make it better?
• Explain several reasons why the characters fit well in this setting.
• Explain several reasons why the characters might fit better in a new setting.
• What makes this setting predictable or unpredictable?
• What setting would make the story more exciting? Explain.
• What setting would make the story dull? Explain.
• Why is the setting important to the story?

Character
• What is the likelihood that the character will…
• Form a hypothesis about what might happen to the character if…
• In what ways did the character show his/her thoughts by his/her actions?
• How might you have done this differently than the character?
• What are some possible explanations for the character's decisions about…
• Explain several reasons why the characters fit well in this setting.
• Explain several reasons why the characters don't fit well in this setting.
• What are some ways you would improve this character's description?
• Predict what the character will do next. Explain.
• What makes this character believable?
• For what reasons do you like or dislike this character?
• What makes this character memorable?
• What is the character thinking?

Teaching Suggestions *(cont.)*

Strategies for Higher-Order Thinking *(cont.)*

Plot

- How does this event affect…
- Predict the outcome…
- What other outcomes could have been possible, and why?
- What problems does this create?
- What is the likelihood…
- Propose a solution.
- Form a hypothesis.
- What is the theme of this story?
- What is the moral of this story?
- What lessons could this story teach us?
- How is this story similar to other stories you have read?
- How is this story similar to other movies you have watched?
- What sequel could result from this story?

Language Usage

- Describe the ways in which the author used language to…
- In what ways did language usage…
- What is the best description of…
- How would you have described this differently?
- What is a better way of describing this, and what makes it better?
- How can you improve upon the word selection…
- How can you improve upon the description of…
- What other words could be substituted for…
- What pictures do the words paint in your mind?
- How do the words set the mood or tone?
- Why would the author decide to use…
- What are some comparisons you could add to…
- In what ways could you add exaggeration to this sentence?

Teaching Suggestions (cont.)

Reading Strategies for Literature

The college and career readiness anchor standards within the Common Core State Standards in reading (National Governors Association Center for Best Practices and Council of Chief State School Officers 2010) include understanding key ideas and details, recognizing craft and structure, and being able to integrate knowledge and ideas. The following two pages offer practical strategies for achieving these standards using the texts found in this book.

Identifying Key Ideas and Details

- Have students work together to create talking tableaux based on parts of the text that infer information. A tableau is a freeze-frame where students are asked to pose and explain the scene from the text they are depicting. As students stand still, they take turns breaking away from the tableau to tell what is being inferred at that moment and how they know this. While this strategy is good for all students, it is a strong activity for **English language learners** because they have an opportunity for encoding and decoding with language and actions.

- Theme is the lesson that the story teaches its readers. It can be applied to everyone, not just the characters in the story. Have students identify the theme and write about what happens that results in their conclusions. Ask students to make connections as to how they can apply the theme to their lives. Allow **below-grade-level** writers to record this information, use graphic organizers for structure, or illustrate their answers in order to make the information more concrete for them.

- Have students draw a picture of the character during an important scene in the story, and use thought bubbles to show the character's secret thoughts based on specific details found in the text. This activity can benefit everyone, but it is very effective for **below-grade-level** writers and **English language learners**. Offering students an opportunity to draw their answers provides them with a creative method to communicate their ideas.

- Have students create before-and-after pictures that show how the characters change over the course of the story. Encourage **above-grade-level** students to examine characters' personality traits and how the characters' thoughts change. This activity encourages students to think about the rationale behind the personality traits they assigned to each character.

Teaching Suggestions *(cont.)*

Reading Strategies for Literature *(cont.)*

Understanding Craft and Structure

- Ask students to identify academic vocabulary in the texts and to practice using the words in a meet-and-greet activity in the classroom, walking around and having conversations using them. This gives **English language learners** an opportunity to practice language acquisition in an authentic way.

- Have students create mini-posters that display the figurative language used in the story. This strategy encourages **below-grade-level** students to show what they have learned.

- Allow students to work in pairs to draw sets of stairs on large paper, and then write how each part of the story builds on the previous part and fits together to provide the overall structure of the story. Homogeneously partner students so that **above-grade-level** students will challenge one another.

- Select at least two or three texts, and have students compare the point of view from which the different stories are narrated. Then, have students change the point of view (e.g., if the story is written in first person, have students rewrite a paragraph in third person). This is a challenging activity specifically suited for **on-grade-level** and **above-grade-level** students to stimulate higher-order thinking.

- Pose the following questions to students: What if the story is told from a different point of view? How does that change the story? Have students select another character's point of view and brainstorm lists of possible changes. This higher-order thinking activity is open-ended and effective for **on-level**, **above-level**, **below-level**, and **English language learners**.

Integrating Knowledge and Ideas

- Show students a section from a movie, a play, or a reader's theater about the story. Have students use graphic organizers to compare and contrast parts of the text with scenes from one of these other sources. Such visual displays support comprehension for **below-level** and **English language learners**.

- Have students locate several illustrations in the text, and then rate the illustrations based on their effective visuals. This higher-order thinking activity is open-ended and is great for **on-level**, **below-level**, **above-level**, and **English language learners**.

- Let students create playlists of at least five songs to go with the mood and tone of the story. Then instruct students to give an explanation for each chosen song. Musically inclined students tend to do very well with this type of activity. It also gives a reason for writing, which can engage **below-grade-level** writers.

- Have students partner up to create talk show segments that discuss similar themes found in the story. Each segment should last between one and two minutes and can be performed live or taped. Encourage students to use visuals, props, and other tools to make it real. Be sure to homogeneously group students for this activity and aid your **below-level** students so they can be successful. This activity allows for **all students** to bring their creative ideas to the table and positively contribute to the end result.

Teaching Suggestions *(cont.)*

Fiction as a Model for Writing

It is only natural that reading and writing go hand in hand in students' literacy development. Both are important for functioning in the real world as adults. Established pieces of fiction, like the ones in this book, serve as models for how to write effectively. After students read the texts in this book, take time for writing instruction. Below are some ideas for writing mini-lessons that can be taught using the texts from this book as writing exemplars.

How to Begin Writing a Story

Instead of beginning a story with '*Once upon a time*' or '*Long, long ago,*' teach students to mimic the styles of well-known authors. As students begin writing projects, show them a variety of first sentences or paragraphs written by different authors. Discuss how these selections are unique. Encourage students to change or adapt the types of beginnings found in the models to make their own story hooks.

Using Good Word Choice

Good word choice can make a significant difference in writing. Help students paint vivid word pictures by showing them examples within the passages found in this book. Instead of writing *I live in a beautiful house,* students can write *I live in a yellow-framed house with black shutters and white pillars that support the wraparound porch.* Encourage students to understand that writing is enriched with sensory descriptions that include what the characters smell, hear, taste, touch, and see. Make students aware of setting the emotional tone in their stories. For example, *In an instant, the hair on the back of his neck stood up, the door creaked open, and a hand reached through.* This example sets a scary mood. Hyperbole is also a great tool to use for effect in stories.

Character Names Can Have Meaning

Students can use names to indicate clues about their characters' personalities. Mrs. Strict could be a teacher, Dr. Molar could be a dentist, and Butch could be the class bully. Remind students that the dialogue between their characters should be real, not forced. Students should think about how people really talk and write dialogue using jargon and colorful words, for example, *"Hey you little twerp, come back here!" yelled Brutus.*

How to Use This Book

Classroom Management for Leveled Texts

Determining your students' instructional reading levels is the first step in the process of effectively managing the leveled-text passages. It is important to assess their reading abilities often so they do not get stuck on one level. Below are suggested ways to use this resource, as well as other resources available to you, to determine students' reading levels.

Running records: While your class is doing independent work, pull your below-grade-level students aside one at a time. Have them individually read aloud the lowest level of a text (the star level) as you record any errors they make on your own copy of the text. Assess their accuracy and fluency, mark the words they say incorrectly, and listen for fluent reading. Use your judgment to determine whether students seem frustrated as they read. If students read accurately and fluently and comprehend the material, move them up to the next level and repeat the process. Following the reading, ask comprehension questions to assess their understanding of the material. As a general guideline, students reading below 90 percent accuracy are likely to feel frustrated as they read. A variety of other published reading assessment tools are available to assess students' reading levels with the running-records format.

Refer to other resources: Another way to determine instructional reading levels is to check your students' Individualized Education Plans; ask the school's language development specialists and/or special education teachers; or review test scores. All of these resources can provide the additional information needed to determine students' reading levels.

How to Use This Book *(cont.)*

Distributing the Texts

Some teachers wonder about how to distribute the different-leveled texts within the classroom. They worry that students will feel insulted or insecure if they do not get the same material as their neighbors. Prior to distributing the texts, make sure that the classroom environment is one in which all students learn at their individual instructional levels. It is important to make this clear. Otherwise, students may constantly ask why their work is different from another student's work. Simply state that students will not be working on the same assignment every day and that their work may slightly vary to resolve students' curiosity. In this approach, distribution of the texts can be very open and causal, just like passing out any other assignment.

Teachers who would rather not have students aware of the differences in the texts can try the suggestions below:

- Make a pile in your hands from star to triangle. Put your finger between the circle and square levels. As you approach each student, pull from the top (star), above your finger (circle), below your finger (square), or the bottom (triangle), depending on each student's level. If you do not hesitate too much in front of each desk, students will probably not notice.

- Begin the class period with an opening activity. Put the texts in different places around the room. As students work quietly, circulate and direct students to the right locations for retrieving the texts you want them to use.

- Organize the texts in small piles by seating arrangement so that when you arrive at a group of desks, you will have only the levels you need.

How to Use This Book (cont.)

Components of the Product

Each passage is derived from classic literary selections. Classics expose readers to cultural heritage or the literature of a culture. Classics improve understanding of the past and, in turn, understanding of the present. These selections from the past explain how we got to where we are today.

The Levels

There are 15 passages in this book, each from a different work of classic fiction. Each passage is leveled to four different reading levels. The images and fonts used for each level within a work of fiction look the same.

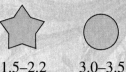

1.5–2.2   3.0–3.5

Behind each page number, you will see a shape. These shapes indicate the reading levels of each piece so that you can make sure students are working with the correct texts. The chart on the following page provides specific levels of each text.

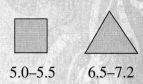

5.0–5.5   6.5–7.2

Leveling Process

The texts in this series are excerpts from classic pieces of literature. A reading specialist has reviewed each excerpt and leveled each one to create four distinct reading passages with unique levels.

Elements of Fiction Question

Each text includes one comprehension question that directs the students to think about the chosen element of fiction for that passage. These questions are written at the appropriate reading level to allow all students to successfully participate in a whole-class discussion. These questions are open-ended and designed to stimulate higher-order thinking.

Digital Resource CD

The Digital Resource CD allows for easy access to all the reading passages in this book. Electronic PDF files as well as word files are included on the CD.

How to Use This Book (cont.)

Title	ELL Level	Below Level	On level	Above level
Setting Passages	☆ 1.5–2.2	◯ 3.0–3.5	▢ 5.0–5.5	△ 6.5–7.2
The Adventures of Pinocchio	2.0	3.5*	5.1	6.5
Mother Goose in Prose	2.2	3.5	5.0	7.2*
Denslow's Three Bears	2.2	3.3	5.5	7.0*
Character Passages				
Alice's Adventures in Wonderland	2.2	3.3	5.0*	6.6
Anne of Green Gables	2.2	3.3	5.3*	6.5
The Magic Fishbone: A Holiday Romance from the Pen of Miss Alice Rainbird	2.2	3.0	5.0*	6.5
The Book of Nature Myths: Why the Bear Has a Short Tail	2.1	3.3*	5.1	6.5
Plot Passages				
The Bremen Town Musicians	2.2	3.3	5.5	7.0*
Clever Else	2.2	3.4	5.5	7.2*
The Story of Doctor Dolittle	1.5	3.0	5.4*	6.5
Tales from Shakespeare	2.1	3.0	5.5	6.5*
Language Usage Passages				
The Celebrated Jumping Frog of Calaveras County	2.2	3.5	5.1	7.0*
How the Camel Got His Hump	2.2	3.5	5.2*	6.8
My Father's Dragon	2.0	3.1	5.0*	6.5
The Wonderful Wizard of Oz	1.7	3.0	5.0*	6.5

* The passages with an asterisk indicate the reading passage from the original work of fiction.

Correlations to Standards

Shell Education is committed to producing educational materials that are research and standards based. In this effort, we have correlated all our products to the academic standards of all 50 United States, the District of Columbia, the Department of Defense Dependent Schools, and all Canadian provinces.

How to Find Standards Correlations

To print a customized correlations report of this product for your state, visit our website at **http://www.shelleducation.com** and follow the on-screen directions. If you require assistance in printing correlations reports, please contact Customer Service at 1-800-858-7339.

Purpose and Intent of Standards

Legislation mandates that all states adopt academic standards that identify the skills students will learn in kindergarten through grade twelve. Many states also have standards for pre-K. This same legislation sets requirements to ensure the standards are detailed and comprehensive.

Standards are designed to focus instruction and guide adoption of curricula. Standards are statements that describe the criteria necessary for students to meet specific academic goals. They define the knowledge, skills, and content students should acquire at each level. Standards are also used to develop standardized tests to evaluate students' academic progress.

Teachers are required to demonstrate how their lessons meet state standards. State standards are used in the development of all our products, so educators can be assured they meet the academic requirements of each state.

McREL Compendium

We use the Mid-continent Research for Education and Learning (McREL) Compendium to create standards correlations. Each year, McREL analyzes state standards and revises the compendium. By following this procedure, McREL is able to produce a general compilation of national standards. Each lesson in this product is based on one or more McREL standards. The chart on the following pages lists each standard taught in this product and the page numbers for the corresponding lessons.

TESOL Standards

The lessons in this book promote English language development for English language learners. The standards listed on the following pages support the language objectives presented throughout the lessons.

Common Core State Standards

The texts in this book are aligned to the Common Core State Standards (CCSS). The standards correlation can be found on pages 28–29.

Correlations to Standards *(cont.)*

Correlation to Common Core State Standards

The passages in this book are aligned to the Common Core State Standards (CCSS). Students who meet these standards develop the skills in reading that are the foundation for any creative and purposeful expression in language.

Grade(s)	Standard
3	RL.3.10—By the end of year, independently and proficiently read and comprehend literature, including stories, dramas, and poetry, at the high end of the grades 2–3 text-complexity band
4–5	RL.4.10–5.10—By the end of the year, proficiently read and comprehend literature, including stories, dramas, and poetry, in the grades 4–5 text-complexity band, with scaffolding as needed at the high end of the range
6–8	RL.6.10–8.10—By the end of the year, proficiently read and comprehend literature, including stories, dramas, and poems, in the grades 6–8 text-complexity band, with scaffolding as needed at the high end of the range.

As outlined by the Common Core State Standards, teachers are "free to provide students with whatever tools and knowledge their professional judgment and experience identify as most helpful for meeting the goals set out in the standards." Bearing this in mind, teachers are encouraged to use the recommendations indicated in the chart below in order to meet additional CCSS Reading Standards that require further instruction.

Standard	Additional Instruction
RL.3.1–5.1— Key Ideas and Details	• Ask and answer questions to demonstrate understanding of a text. • Refer to details and examples in a text. • Quote accurately from a text when explaining what the text says.
RL.3.2–5.2— Key Ideas and Details	• Recount stories to determine the central message, lesson, or moral and explain how it is conveyed. • Determine a theme of a story from details in the text.
RL.3.3–5.3— Key Ideas and Details	• Describe in depth a character, setting, or event in a story.
RL.6.1–8.1— Key Ideas and Details	• Cite textual evidence to support analysis of what the text says.
RL.6.2–8.2— Key Ideas and Details	• Determine a theme or central idea of a text and analyze its development over the course of the text.
RL.6.3–8.3— Key Ideas and Details	• Analyze how particular elements of a story or drama interact.

Correlations to Standards (cont.)

Correlation to Common Core State Standards (cont.)

Standard	Additional Instruction (cont.)
RL.3.4–8.4—Craft and Structure	• Determine the meaning of words and phrases as they are used in the text.
RL.3.5–5.5—Craft and Structure	• Refer to parts of stories when writing or speaking about a text. • Explain the overall structure of a story.
RL.3.6–8.6—Craft and Structure	• Distinguish and describe point of view within the story.
RL.6.5–8.5—Craft and Structure	• Analyze and compare and contrast the overall structure of a story.
RL.3.7–5.7—Integration of Knowledge and Ideas	• Explain how specific aspects of a text's illustrations contribute to what is conveyed by the words in a story.
RL.3.9–8.9—Integration of Knowledge and Ideas	• Compare and contrast the themes, settings, and plots of stories.

Correlation to McREL Standards

Standard	Page(s)
5.1—Previews text (3–5)	all
5.1—Establishes and adjusts purposes for reading (6–8)	all
5.2—Establishes and adjusts purposes for reading (3–5)	all
5.3—Makes, confirms, and revises simple predictions about what will be found in a text (3–5)	all
5.3—Uses a variety of strategies to extend reading vocabulary (6–8)	all
5.4—Uses specific strategies to clear up confusing parts of a text (6–8)	all
5.5—Use a variety of context clues to decode unknown words (3–5)	all
5.5—Understands specific devices an author uses to accomplish his or her purpose (6–8)	all
5.6—Reflects on what has been learned after reading and formulates ideas, opinions, and personal responses to texts (6–8)	all

Correlation to Standards *(cont.)*

Correlation to McREL Standards *(cont.)*

Standard	Page(s)
5.7—Understands level-appropriate reading vocabulary (3–5)	all
5.8—Monitors own reading strategies and makes modifications as needed (3–5)	all
5.10—Understands the author's purpose or point of view (3–5)	all
6.1—Reads a variety of literary passages and texts (3–5, 6–8)	all
6.2—Knows the defining characteristics and structural elements of a variety of literary genres (3–5, 6–8)	all
6.3—Understands the basic concept of plot (3–5)	all
6.3—Understands complex elements of plot development (6–8)	all
6.4—Understands similarities and differences within and among literary works from various genres and cultures (3–5)	all
6.4—Understands elements of character development (6–8)	all
6.5—Understands elements of character development in literary works (3–5)	all
6.7—Understands the ways in which language is used in literary texts (3–5)	all

Correlation to TESOL Standards

Standard	Page(s)
2.1—Students will use English to interact in the classroom	all
2.2—Students will use English to obtain, process, construct, and provide subject matter information in spoken and written form	all
2.3—Students will use appropriate learning strategies to construct and apply academic knowledge	all

Excerpt from

The Adventures of Pinocchio

by C. Collodi

[*Mastro "Cherry" Antonio is a carpenter. He has found a strange piece of wood.*]

He gave the wood a hard knock. "Oh, oh! You hurt!" cried a faraway little voice.

Mastro Cherry grew dumb. His eyes popped out of his head. His mouth opened wide. His tongue hung down on his chin. He was trembling. He was stuttering from fright. But, as soon as he got the use of his senses, he said:

"Where did that voice come from? There is no one around! Might it be that this piece of wood has learned to weep and cry like a child? I can hardly believe it. Here it is. It is a piece of common firewood. It is good only to burn in the stove. It is just like any other. Yet—might someone be hidden in it? If so, the worse for him. I'll fix him!"

With these words, he grabbed the log with both hands. He started to knock it about unmercifully. He threw it to the floor. He threw it against the walls of the room. He even threw it up to the ceiling.

He listened for the tiny voice to moan and cry. He waited two minutes—nothing. He waited five minutes—nothing. Ten minutes passed—still nothing.

"Oh, I see," he said. He was trying bravely to laugh. He ruffled up his wig with his hand. "I only imagined I heard the tiny voice! Well, well—to work once more!"

The poor fellow was scared half to death. So he tried to sing a happy song to gain courage. He set aside the hatchet. He picked up the plane to make the wood smooth and even. But as he drew it to and fro, he heard the same tiny voice. This time it giggled as it spoke:

"Stop it! Oh, stop it! Ha, ha, ha! You tickle my stomach."

This time poor Mastro Cherry fell as if shot. When he opened his eyes, he found himself sitting on the floor. His face had changed. Fright had turned even the tip of his nose from red to deepest purple. In that very instant, a loud knock sounded on the door. "Come in," said the carpenter. He did not have even an atom of strength left with which to stand up.

At the words, the door opened. A dapper little old man came in. His name was Geppetto. But to the boys of the neighborhood he was Polendina (*cornmeal mush*). This was on account of the wig he always wore which was just the color of yellow corn. Geppetto had a very bad temper. Woe to the one who called him Polendina! He became as wild as a beast! No one could soothe him.

"Good day, Mastro Antonio," said Geppetto. "What are you doing on the floor?"

"I am teaching the ants their A B C's."

"Good luck to you!"

"What brought you here, friend Geppetto?"

"My legs. And it may flatter you to know, Mastro Antonio, that I have come to you to beg for a favor."

"Here I am, at your service," answered the carpenter. He raised himself on to his knees.

"I thought of making myself a beautiful wooden Marionette. It must be wonderful! It must be able to dance, fence, and turn somersaults. With it I will go around the world to earn my crust of bread and cup of wine. What do you think of it?"

Element Focus: Setting

What are some possible explanations
for selecting this setting?

#50988—*Leveled Texts for Classic Fiction: Humor*

Excerpt from

The Adventures of Pinocchio

by C. Collodi

[*Mastro "Cherry" Antonio is a carpenter who has found a strange little log.*]

He struck a most solemn blow upon the piece of wood. "Oh, oh! You hurt!" cried a faraway little voice.

Mastro Cherry grew dumb, his eyes popped out of his head, his mouth opened wide, and his tongue hung down on his chin. As soon as he regained the use of his senses, he said, trembling and stuttering from fright:

"Where did that voice come from, when there is no one around? Might it be that this piece of wood has learned to weep and cry like a child? I can hardly believe it. Here it is—a piece of common firewood, good only to burn in the stove, the same as any other. Yet—might someone be hidden in it? If so, the worse for him. I'll fix him!"

With these words, he grabbed the log with both hands and started to knock it about unmercifully. He threw it to the floor, against the walls of the room, and even up to the ceiling.

He listened for the tiny voice to moan and cry. He waited two minutes—nothing; five minutes—nothing; ten minutes—nothing.

"Oh, I see," he said, trying bravely to laugh and ruffling up his wig with his hand. "It can easily be seen I only imagined I heard the tiny voice! Well, well—to work once more!"

The poor fellow was scared half to death, so he tried to sing a happy song in order to gain courage. He set aside the hatchet and picked up the plane to make the wood smooth and even, but as he drew it to and fro, he heard the same tiny voice. This time it giggled as it spoke:

"Stop it! Oh, stop it! Ha, ha, ha! You tickle my stomach."

This time poor Mastro Cherry fell as if shot. When he opened his eyes, he found himself sitting on the floor. His face had changed; fright had turned even the tip of his nose from red to deepest purple. In that very instant, a loud knock sounded on the door. "Come in," said the carpenter, not having an atom of strength left with which to stand up.

At the words, the door opened and a dapper little old man came in. His name was Geppetto, but to the boys of the neighborhood he was Polendina (*cornmeal mush*), on account of the wig he always wore which was just the color of yellow corn. Geppetto had a very bad temper. Woe to the one who called him Polendina! He became as wild as a beast and no one could soothe him.

"Good day, Mastro Antonio," said Geppetto. "What are you doing on the floor?"

"I am teaching the ants their A B C's."

"Good luck to you!"

"What brought you here, friend Geppetto?"

"My legs. And it may flatter you to know, Mastro Antonio, that I have come to you to beg for a favor."

"Here I am, at your service," answered the carpenter, raising himself on to his knees.

"I thought of making myself a beautiful wooden Marionette. It must be wonderful, one that will be able to dance, fence, and turn somersaults. With it I intend to go around the world, to earn my crust of bread and cup of wine. What do you think of it?"

Element Focus: Setting

Why is the setting important to the story?

Excerpt from

The Adventures of Pinocchio

by C. Collodi

[*Mastro "Cherry" Antonio is a carpenter who has found a strange piece of wood.*]

He struck a most solemn blow upon the piece of wood. "Oh, oh! You hurt!" cried a faraway little voice.

Mastro Cherry grew dumb, his eyes popped out of his head, his mouth opened wide, and his tongue hung down on his chin. As soon as he regained the use of his senses he began to speak, trembling and stuttering from fright:

"Where did that voice come from, when there is no one around? Might it be that this piece of wood has learned to weep and cry like a child? I can hardly believe it. Here it is—a piece of common firewood, good only to burn in the stove, the same as any other. Yet—might someone be hidden inside of it? If so, then it is the worse for him. I'll fix him!"

With these words, he grabbed the log with both hands and started to pummel it and hurl it about unmercifully. He threw it harshly to the floor, against the walls of the room, and even up to the ceiling.

He listened for the tiny voice to moan and cry but didn't hear a peep. He waited two minutes, but there was nothing. At the five minute mark, there was still nothing. Indeed, after 10 minutes the wood was still as silent as any ordinary piece of wood should be.

"Oh, I see," he said, trying bravely to laugh and ruffling up his curly white wig with his hand. "It can easily be seen that I only imagined I heard the tiny voice! Well, well, enough of this nonsense, I must get back to work!"

The poor fellow was frightened half to death, so he tried to sing a happy song in order to gain himself some courage. He set aside the hatchet and picked up the plane to make the wood smooth and even, but as he drew it to and fro, he heard the same tiny voice, this time giggling as it spoke:

"Stop it! Oh, stop it! Ha, ha, ha! You tickle my stomach."

This time poor Mastro Cherry fell as if shot, and when he reopened his eyes, he discovered that he was sitting on the floor. His face had changed with the shock of the fright, turning even the tip of his nose from red to deepest purple. In that very instant, a loud knock sounded on the door. "Please enter," said the carpenter, not having an atom of strength left with which to even stand up.

At the words, the door opened and a dapper little old man came in. His name was Geppetto, but to the boys of the neighborhood he was Polendina (*cornmeal mush*), on account of the wig he always wore which was just the color of yellow corn. Geppetto had an extremely volatile temper indeed. Woe to the one who called him Polendina, because Geppetto would become as wild as a beast and no one could soothe him.

"Good day, Mastro Antonio," said Geppetto cheerfully enough. "What, pray tell, are you doing on the floor?"

"I am teaching the ants their A B C's," replied the carpenter from his compromised position near the other man's feet.

"Good luck to you!" replied Geppetto with good humor.

"What brought you here, friend Geppetto?" inquired Mastro Cherry, regaining some of his composure.

"My legs. And it may flatter you to know, Mastro Antonio, that I have come to you to beg for a favor."

"Here I am, completely at your service," answered the carpenter, raising himself on to his knees in a preliminary effort to stand.

"I am considering making myself a beautiful wooden Marionette. It must be wonderful, one that will be able to dance, fence, and turn somersaults. With it I intend to go around the world, performing to earn my crust of bread and cup of wine. What do you think of it?"

Element Focus: Setting

What new element would you add
to this setting to make it better?

The Adventures of Pinocchio

by C. Collodi

[*Mastro "Cherry" Antonio is a carpenter who has found a strange little wooden log.*]

Mastro Cherry struck a most solemn blow upon the piece of wood. "Oh, oh! You hurt!" cried a faraway little voice.

Mastro Cherry grew dumb, his eyes popped out of his head, his mouth opened wide, and his tongue hung down on his chin. As soon as he regained the use of his senses he began to speak, trembling and stuttering from fright:

"Where did that voice come from, when there is no one around? Might it be that this piece of wood has learned to weep and cry like a child? I can hardly believe it. Here it is—a piece of common firewood, suitable only to burn in the stove, the same as any other. Yet—might someone perhaps be concealed inside of it? If so, then it is the worse for him because I will soon cook his goose!"

With these words, he grabbed the log with both hands and started to pummel it and hurl it about unmercifully. He threw it forcefully to the floor, walloped it against the walls of the room, and even launched it vigorously up to the ceiling.

He listened for the tiny voice to moan and cry but didn't hear a peep. He waited two minutes, but all was peaceful. At the five minute mark, there was still nothing. Indeed, after 10 minutes the log remained as silent as any ordinary hunk of wood should be.

"Oh, I understand now," he said, trying courageously to laugh and ruffling up his curly white wig with his hand. "It is obvious that I only imagined I heard the tiny voice! Well, well, enough of this nonsense, I must get back to work!"

The poor fellow was frightened half to death, so he tried to sing a happy song in order to gain himself some courage. He set aside the hatchet and picked up the plane to make the wood smooth and even, but as he drew it to and fro, he heard the same tiny voice, this time giggling as it spoke:

"Stop it! Oh, stop it! Ha, ha, ha! You tickle my stomach."

This time poor Mastro Cherry fell as if shot, and upon reopening his eyes, he discovered that he was sitting on the floor. His face had changed with the shock of the fright, turning even the tip of his nose from red to deepest purple. In that very instant, a loud knock sounded on the door. "Please enter," called the carpenter, not having an atom of strength left with which to even stand.

At the words, the door sprang open and a dapper little old man came in. His name was Geppetto, but to the boys of the neighborhood he was Polendina (*cornmeal mush*), on account of the yellow wig he always wore which was just the color of corn. Geppetto was afflicted with an extremely volatile temper. Woe to the one who called him Polendina, because Geppetto would become as wild as a beast and no one could soothe him.

"Good day, Mastro Antonio," said Geppetto cheerfully enough. "What, pray tell, are you doing on the floor?"

"I am teaching the ants their A B C's," replied the carpenter innocently from his compromised position near the old gentleman's feet.

"Good luck to you!" replied Geppetto with good humor.

"What brought you here, friend Geppetto?" inquired Mastro Cherry, regaining some of his composure.

"Why, my legs of course. And it may flatter you to know, Mastro Antonio, that I have come to you to entreat a favor," the crisply dressed Geppetto replied, still smiling agreeably.

"Here I am, completely at your service," answered the carpenter, raising himself on to his knees in a preliminary effort to stand.

"I am considering making myself a beautiful wooden Marionette. It must be wonderful, one that will be able to dance, fence, and turn somersaults," revealed Geppetto with a theatrical flourish. "With it I intend to go around the world, performing to earn my crust of bread and cup of wine. What do you think of it?"

Element Focus: Setting

Explain why the characters fit well in this setting.

Excerpt from

Mother Goose in Prose

by L. Frank Baum

The Man in the moon came tumbling down,1
And enquired the way to Norwich;
He went by the south and burned his mouth
With eating cold pease porridge!

Everything went by opposites in the moon. When the Man wanted to keep warm, he put chunks of ice in his stove. He cooled his drinking water by throwing red-hot coals of fire into the pitcher. When he got chilly, he took off his hat and coat. He might even remove his shoes. This would make him toasty warm. In the hot days of summer, he put on his overcoat to cool off.

Well, he sat by his ice-cool fire and thought about his trip to Earth. He decided the only way he could get there was to slide down a moonbeam. So, he went to the edge of the moon. He began to look for a good strong moonbeam.

At last he found one that seemed sturdy. It reached right down to a pleasant-looking spot on the earth. So he swung himself over the edge of the moon. He put both arms tight around the moonbeam. Then he started to slide down. But it was slippery! He tried to hold tight. But, he found himself going faster and faster. Just before he reached the earth, he lost his hold! He came tumbling down head over heels. Plump! He fell into a river.

The cool water nearly burned him! But luckily he was near the bank. He quickly scrambled upon the land. Then he sat down to catch his breath.

Soon a farmer came along the road. He had a team of horses pulling a load of hay. The horses looked very strange to the Man in the moon! At first he was very afraid. He had never seen horses except from his home in the moon. And from up there they looked much smaller. But he plucked up courage. He said to the farmer, "Can you tell me the way to Norwich, sir?"

"Norwich?" said the farmer thoughtfully. "I don't know exactly where it is, sir. But it's somewhere away to the south."

"Thank you," said the Man in the moon. But stop! I must not call him the Man in the moon now. He is not in the moon anymore. So, I'll just call him the Man. You'll know by that which man I mean.

Well, the Man in the—I mean the Man (I nearly forgot what I just said)—the Man turned to the south. He began walking. He had made up his mind to do as the alderman had advised. He planned to travel to Norwich. There he would eat some of the famous pease porridge. After a long and tiresome journey, he reached the town. He stopped at one of the first houses he came to. By this time he was very hungry!

A good-looking woman answered his knock at the door. He asked politely, "Is this the town of Norwich, madam?"

"Surely this is the town of Norwich," returned the woman.

"I came here to see if I could get some pease porridge," continued the Man. "I hear you make the nicest porridge in the world in this town."

"That we do, sir," said the woman. "If you'll step inside, I'll give you a bowl. I have plenty in the house. And it is newly made."

Element Focus: Setting

Describe the ways that the moon is different than Earth in the story.

Excerpt from

Mother Goose in Prose

by L. Frank Baum

The Man in the moon came tumbling down,
And enquired the way to Norwich;
He went by the south and burned his mouth
With eating cold pease porridge!

You see, everything went by opposites in the moon. When the Man wished to keep warm, he knocked off a few chunks of ice and put them in his stove. He cooled his drinking water by throwing red-hot coals of fire into the pitcher. When he became chilly, he took off his hat and coat. He might even remove his shoes. This would make him toasty warm. In the hot days of summer, he put on his overcoat to cool off.

Well, he sat by his ice-cool fire and thought about his trip to Earth. Finally, he decided the only way he could get there was to slide down a moonbeam. So, he went to the edge of the moon and began to look for a good strong moonbeam.

At last he found one that seemed sturdy. It reached right down to a pleasant-looking spot on the earth. So he swung himself over the edge of the moon. He put both arms tight around the moonbeam and started to slide down. But he found it rather slippery! In spite of all his efforts to hold on, he found himself going faster and faster. So, just before he reached the earth, he lost his hold. He came tumbling down head over heels and fell plump into a river.

The cool water nearly burned him before he could swim out. But fortunately he was near the bank. He quickly scrambled upon the land. He sat down to catch his breath.

By and by a farmer came along the road by the river with a team of horses drawing a load of hay. The horses looked so odd to the Man in the moon that at first, he was greatly frightened, never before having seen horses except from his home on the moon. And from there they looked a good deal smaller. But he plucked up courage and said to the farmer, "Can you tell me the way to Norwich, sir?"

"Norwich?" repeated the farmer musingly. "I don't know exactly where it be, sir, but it's somewhere away to the south."

"Thank you," said the Man in the moon. But stop! I must not call him the Man in the moon any longer. For of course he was now out of the moon. So, I'll simply call him the Man. You'll know by that which man I mean.

Well, the Man in the—I mean the Man (but I nearly forgot what I have just said)—the Man turned to the south and began walking briskly along the road. He had made up his mind to do as the alderman had advised. He planned to travel to Norwich. And there he would eat some of the famous pease porridge. After a long and tiresome journey, he reached the town and stopped at one of the first houses he came to. By this time he was very hungry indeed.

A good-looking woman answered his knock at the door. He asked politely, "Is this the town of Norwich, madam?"

"Surely this is the town of Norwich," returned the woman.

"I came here to see if I could get some pease porridge," continued the Man. "For I hear you make the nicest porridge in the world in this town."

"That we do, sir," answered the woman. "If you'll step inside, I'll give you a bowl. I have plenty in the house that is newly made."

Element Focus: Setting

Predict the outcome if the Man in the moon were to drink a cup of hot tea.

Excerpt from

Mother Goose in Prose

by L. Frank Baum

The Man in the moon came tumbling down,
And enquired the way to Norwich;
He went by the south and burned his mouth
With eating cold pease porridge!

You see, everything went by contraries in the moon. When the Man wished to keep warm, he knocked off a few chunks of ice and put them in his stove. He cooled his drinking water by throwing red-hot coals of fire into the pitcher. Likewise, when he became chilly, he took off his hat and coat, and even his shoes, and so became warm. And in the hot days of summer, he put on his overcoat to cool off.

Well, he sat by his ice-cool fire and thought about his journey to Earth. Finally, he decided the only way he could get there was to slide down a moonbeam. So, he went to the edge of the moon and began to search for a good strong moonbeam.

At last he found one that seemed rather substantial and reached right down to a pleasant-looking spot on the earth. So he swung himself over the edge of the moon, and put both arms tight around the moonbeam and started to slide down. But he found it rather slippery! In spite of all his efforts to hold on, he found himself going faster and faster. So, just before he reached the earth, he lost his hold and came tumbling down head over heels and fell plump into a river.

The cool water nearly scalded him before he could swim out. But fortunately he was near the bank and he rapidly scrambled upon the land and sat down to catch his breath.

By and by a farmer came along the road by the river with a team of horses drawing a load of hay. The horses looked so odd to the Man in the Moon that at first, he was greatly frightened, never before having seen horses except from his home on the moon. And from there they looked a good deal smaller. But he plucked up courage and said to the farmer,

"Can you tell me the way to Norwich, sir?"

"Norwich?" repeated the farmer musingly. "I don't know exactly where it be, sir, but it's somewhere away to the south."

"Thank you," said the Man in the moon. But stop! I must not call him the Man in the moon any longer. For of course he was now out of the moon. So, I'll modestly call him the Man, and you'll know by that which man I mean.

Well, the Man in the—I mean the Man (but I nearly forgot what I have just said)—the Man turned to the south and began walking briskly along the road. He had made up his mind to do as the alderman had advised. He planned to travel to Norwich. And there he would eat some of the famous pease porridge. After a long and tiresome journey, he reached the town and stopped at one of the first houses he came to. By this time he was very hungry indeed.

A good-looking woman answered his knock at the door. He asked politely, "Is this the town of Norwich, madam?"

"Surely this is the town of Norwich," returned the woman.

"I came here to see if I could get some pease porridge," continued the Man. "For I hear you make the nicest porridge in the world in this town."

"That we do, sir," answered the woman. "If you'll step inside, I'll give you a bowl, for I have plenty in the house that is newly made."

Element Focus: Setting

Describe three ways in which the moon is different than Earth.

Excerpt from

Mother Goose in Prose

by L. Frank Baum

The Man in the moon came tumbling down,
And enquired the way to Norwich;
He went by the south and burned his mouth
With eating cold pease porridge!

You see, everything went by contraries in the moon, and when the Man wished to keep warm he knocked off a few chunks of ice and put them in his stove. He cooled his drinking water by throwing red-hot coals of fire into the pitcher. Likewise, when he became chilly he took off his hat and coat, and even his shoes, and so became warm. And in the hot days of summer he put on his overcoat to cool off.

Well, he sat by his ice-cool fire and thought about his journey to the earth, and finally he decided the only way he could get there was to slide down a moonbeam. So, he went to the edge of the moon and began to search for a good strong moonbeam.

At last he found one that seemed rather substantial and reached right down to a pleasant-looking spot on the earth. And so he swung himself over the edge of the moon, and put both arms tight around the moonbeam and started to slide down. But he found it rather slippery, and in spite of all his efforts to hold on he found himself going faster and faster, so that just before he reached the earth he lost his hold and came tumbling down head over heels and fell plump into a river.

The cool water nearly scalded him before he could swim out, but fortunately he was near the bank and he quickly scrambled upon the land and sat down to catch his breath.

By and by a farmer came along the road by the river with a team of horses drawing a load of hay, and the horses looked so odd to the Man in the moon that at first he was greatly frightened, never before having seen horses except from his home in the moon, from whence they looked a good deal smaller. But he plucked up courage and said to the farmer,

"Can you tell me the way to Norwich, sir?"

"Norwich?" repeated the farmer musingly; "I don't know exactly where it be, sir, but it's somewhere away to the south."

"Thank you," said the Man in the moon. But stop! I must not call him the Man in the Moon any longer, for of course he was now out of the moon. So, I'll simply call him the Man, and you'll know by that which man I mean.

Well, the Man in the—I mean the Man (but I nearly forgot what I have just said)—the Man turned to the south and began walking briskly along the road, for he had made up his mind to do as the alderman had advised and travel to Norwich, that he might eat some of the famous pease porridge that was made there. And finally, after a long and tiresome journey, he reached the town and stopped at one of the first houses he came to, for by this time he was very hungry indeed.

A good-looking woman answered his knock at the door, and he asked politely, "Is this the town of Norwich, madam?"

"Surely this is the town of Norwich," returned the woman.

"I came here to see if I could get some pease porridge," continued the Man, "for I hear you make the nicest porridge in the world in this town."

"That we do, sir," answered the woman. "If you'll step inside I'll give you a bowl, for I have plenty in the house that is newly made."

Element Focus: Setting

In what ways do the differences between the moon and Earth contribute to the humor of the story?

Excerpt from

Denslow's Three Bears

adapted by W. W. Denslow

A long time ago there was a great forest. At the edge of the woods was a little cottage. In it lived a little girl by the name of Golden Hair. She was an orphan. And she lived with her grandmother who loved her dearly. The grandmother was very old. So most of the housework was done by Golden Hair. But she was young and strong. She did not mind it one bit. She still had plenty of time to play. She was merry the whole day long.

Little Golden Hair lived far from other children. But she was never lonesome. She had many friends in the wild creatures of the wood. The gentle, soft-eyed deer would feed from her hand. And the wild birds would come at her musical call. She knew their language. And she loved them well.

Golden Hair had never wandered far into the forest. But one autumn day, she was gathering bright leaves and golden rod. She went farther than she realized. She found a lonely, gray cabin. It was hidden under the huge trees. A slab of wood beside the half open door told who lived there. It read: "Papa Bear, Mamma Bear, and the Tiny Bear."

"So this is where the jolly bears live!" said Golden Hair. She knocked on the door. "I want to meet them."

No one answered. So she pushed the door. It opened wide. She walked in.

It was a very messy house. But there was a bright fire. And over it hung a big, black kettle of bubbling soup. On the table were three yellow bowls. They were all different sizes.

"Here is a big bowl for Papa Bear. Here is a medium sized bowl for Mamma Bear. And here is a little bowl for the Tiny Bear," said Golden Hair.

"That soup smells good," said Golden Hair. "But my! What a messy house! I'll clean up while I am waiting for the bears to come home."

So she went to work. She swept. She dusted. Soon she had the room in order. Then she went into the bedroom. She made up the three beds. She made the big one for Papa Bear. She made the medium one for Mamma Bear. And she made the little one for the Tiny Bear. She worked hard. Everything was neat as a pin when in bounced the three jolly bears. For a moment the bears stood speechless! They stared at Golden Hair with wide-open eyes. The girl stood like a ray of sunshine in the dusky room. Then they burst into loud laughter. They made her welcome to their home. When they saw how nice and clean it was, they thanked her heartily! They invited her to share their dinner. The soup was now ready. And they were all hungry. Golden Hair spent the rest of the day with the three jolly bears. They played "hi spy." The bears taught her many new games.

Soon the afternoon sun was sinking in the west. The little girl said she must be getting home. Her grandma would be worried about her. The three bears would not let her go alone. So they all set off together. They walked merrily through the twilight woods.

Golden Hair rode on Papa Bear's back. Mamma Bear and Tiny walked happily on either side. In this way, before night had fallen, they came clear of the woods. They walked up to the home of Golden Hair.

To be sure, the grandmother was surprised to see this shaggy group with her little Golden Hair. But she saw how jolly they all were. And she noted how handy they were in helping Golden Hair get the supper. So she gave them welcome. She was delighted to have them stay. Papa Bear split the wood. He brought it in, and built the fire. The Tiny bear carried water from the well. And Mamma Bear filled the teakettle with the water. Soon they were able to sit down to a good supper. They had hot biscuits, wild honey, and pumpkin pie. There was tea for the elders and nice sweet milk for Golden Hair and the Tiny Bear.

The grandmother liked the three bears. And the bears were delighted with the comforts of home. So they all decided to live together for the general good.

Element Focus: Setting

Explain why the character of
Golden Hair fits well with this setting.

Excerpt from

Denslow's Three Bears

adapted by W. W. Denslow

A long time ago there was a cottage on the edge of a great forest. In it dwelt a little girl by the name of Golden Hair. She was an orphan. And she lived with her grandmother who loved her dearly. The grandmother was very old. So, most of the housework was done by Golden Hair. But she was so young and strong she did not mind that a bit. She still had plenty of time to play. She was merry the whole day long.

Although little Golden Hair lived far from other children, she was never lonesome. She had many friends in the wild creatures of the wood. The gentle, soft-eyed deer would feed from her hand. And the wild birds would come at her musical call. She knew their language and loved them well.

Golden Hair had never wandered far into the forest. But one day in the early autumn time, she was gathering bright leaves and golden rod. She strayed farther than she knew. She found a lonely, gray cabin under the mighty trees. A slab of wood beside the half open door told who lived there. It read: "Papa Bear, Mamma Bear, and the Tiny Bear."

"So this is where the jolly bears live!" said Golden Hair. She knocked on the door. "I want to meet them."

No answer came to her knocking. So, she pushed the door. It opened wide and she walked in.

It was a very messy house. But a bright fire burned on the hearth. And over it hung a big, black kettle of bubbling soup. On the table were three yellow bowls of different sizes.

"Here is a big bowl for Papa Bear. Here is a medium sized bowl for Mamma Bear. And here is a little bowl for the Tiny Bear," said Golden Hair.

"That soup smells good," she went on to say. "But my! What a messy house! I'll clean up while I am waiting for the bears to come home."

So she went to work. She swept. She dusted. Soon she had the room in order. Then she went into the bedroom. She made up the three beds. She made the big one for Papa Bear. She made the medium one for Mamma Bear. And she made the little one for the Tiny Bear. She bustled and had everything neat as a pin when in bounced the three jolly bears. For a moment the bears stood speechless with wide-open eyes, staring at Golden Hair, who stood, like a ray of sunshine in the dusky room. Then they burst into loud laughter and made her welcome to their home. When they saw how nice and clean it was they thanked her heartily! They invited her to share their dinner. The soup was now ready and they were all hungry. Golden Hair spent the rest of the day with the three jolly bears. They played "hi spy" and many new games that the bears taught her.

When the afternoon sun was sinking in the west, the little girl said she must be getting home. Her grandma would be anxious about her. The three bears would not let her go alone. So they all set off together. They walked merrily through the twilight woods.

Golden Hair rode on the broad back of Papa Bear. Mamma Bear and Tiny strode happily on either side. In this way before night had fallen, they came clear of the woods and up to the home of Golden Hair.

To be sure, the grandmother was much surprised to see this shaggy company with her little Golden Hair. But when she saw how jolly they all were and how handy they were in helping Golden Hair get the supper, she was delighted to have them stay, and gave them welcome. Papa Bear split the wood, brought it in, and built the fire. Mamma Bear got the teakettle and filled it with water that was carried from the well by the Tiny Bear. And soon they were able to sit down to a good supper of hot biscuits, wild honey, and pumpkin pie, with tea for the elders and nice sweet milk for Golden Hair and the Tiny Bear.

The grandmother liked the three bears so well and the bears were so delighted with the comforts of home that they all decided to live together for the general good.

Element Focus: Setting

What makes this setting predictable or unpredictable?

Excerpt from
Denslow's Three Bears

adapted by W. W. Denslow

A long time ago in a cottage on the edge of a great forest, there dwelt a little girl by the name of Golden Hair. She was an orphan and lived with her grandmother who loved her dearly. The grandmother was very old and so most of the housework was done by Golden Hair. But she was so young and strong she did not mind that a bit. She still had plenty of time to play and was merry the whole day long.

Although little Golden Hair lived far from other children, she was never lonesome. She had many friends and playmates in the wild creatures of the wood. The gentle, soft-eyed deer would feed from her hand, and the wild birds would come at her musical call. She knew their language and loved them well.

Golden Hair had never wandered far into the forest. But one day in the early autumn time, as she was gathering bright leaves and golden rod, she strayed farther than she knew. She happened upon a lonely, gray cabin under the mighty trees. A slab of wood beside the half open door told who lived within. It read: "Papa Bear, Mamma Bear, and the Tiny Bear."

"So this is where the jolly bears live!" said Golden Hair, as she knocked upon the door. "I want to meet them."

No answer came to her knocking, so she pushed the door wide open and walked in.

It was a most disorderly house. But a bright fire burned on the hearth, over which hung a big, black kettle of bubbling soup. On the table, nearby, were three yellow bowls of different sizes.

"A big bowl for Papa Bear, a medium sized bowl for Mamma Bear, and a little bowl for the Tiny Bear," said Golden Hair.

"That soup smells good," she went on to say, "But my! What an untidy house! I'll put the place to rights while I am waiting for the bears to come home."

So she went to work to sweep and dust and soon had the room in order. Then she went into the bedroom and made up the three beds. She made the big one for Papa Bear, the medium one for Mamma Bear, and the little one for the Tiny Bear. She bustled and had everything neat as a pin when in bounced the three jolly bears. For a moment the bears stood speechless with wide-open eyes, staring at Golden Hair, who stood, like a ray of sunshine in the dusky room. Then they burst into loud laughter and made her welcome to their home. When they saw how nice and clean it was, they thanked her heartily! They invited her to share their dinner, for the soup was now ready and they were all hungry. Golden Hair spent the rest of the day with the three jolly bears playing "hi spy" and many new games that the bears taught her.

When the afternoon sun was sinking in the west, the little girl said she must be getting home. Her grandma would be anxious about her. The three bears would not let her go alone. So they all set off together through the twilight woods—a merry company.

Golden Hair rode on the broad back of Papa Bear, while Mamma Bear and Tiny Bear strode happily on either side. In this way, before night had fallen, they came clear of the woods and up to the home of Golden Hair.

To be sure, the grandmother was much surprised to see this shaggy company with her little Golden Hair. But when she saw how jolly they all were and how handy they were in helping Golden Hair get the supper, she was delighted to have them stay, and gave them welcome. Papa Bear split the wood, brought it in, and built the fire. Mamma Bear got the teakettle and filled it with water that was carried from the well by the Tiny Bear. And soon they were able to sit down to a good supper of hot biscuits, wild honey, and pumpkin pie, with tea for the elders and nice sweet milk for Golden Hair and the Tiny Bear.

The grandmother liked the three bears so well and the bears were so delighted with the comforts of home that they all decided to live together for the general good.

Element Focus: Setting

Why do you think the author selected this setting?

Excerpt from

Denslow's Three Bears

adapted by W. W. Denslow

A long time ago in a cottage on the edge of a great forest there dwelt a little girl by the name of Golden Hair; she was an orphan and lived with her grandmother who loved her dearly. The grandmother was very old and so most of the house work was done by Golden Hair; but she was so young and strong she did not mind that a bit, for she had plenty of time to play and was merry the whole day long.

Although little Golden Hair lived far from other children she was never lonesome, for she had many friends and playmates in the wild creatures of the wood. The gentle, soft eyed deer would feed from her hand, and the wild birds would come at her musical call; for she knew their language and loved them well.

Golden Hair had never wandered far into the forest. But one day in the early autumn time, as she was gathering bright leaves and golden rod, she strayed farther than she knew and came upon a lonely, gray cabin under the mighty trees. A slab of wood beside the half open door told who lived within. It read: "Papa Bear, Mamma Bear and the Tiny Bear."

"So this is where the jolly bears live!" said Golden Hair, as she knocked upon the door. "I want to meet them."

No answer came to her knocking, so she pushed the door wide open and walked in.

It was a most disorderly house, but a bright fire burned on the hearth, over which hung a big, black kettle of bubbling soup, while on the table, nearby, were three yellow bowls of different sizes.

"A big bowl for Papa Bear, a medium sized bowl for Mamma Bear, and a little bowl for the Tiny Bear," said Golden Hair.

"That soup smells good," she went on to say, "But my! What an untidy house! I'll put the place to rights while I am waiting for the bears to come home."

So she went to work to sweep and dust and soon had the room in order. Then she went into the bed room and made up the three beds: the big one for Papa Bear, the medium one for Mamma Bear, and the little one for the Tiny Bear. She bustled and had everything neat as a pin when in bounced the three jolly bears. For a moment the bears stood speechless with wide open eyes, staring at Golden Hair, who stood, like a ray of sunshine in the dusky room; then they burst into loud laughter and made her welcome to their home. When they saw how nice and clean it was they thanked her heartily and invited her to share their dinner, for the soup was now ready and they were all hungry. Golden Hair spent the rest of the day with the three jolly bears playing "hi spy" and many new games that the bears taught her.

When the afternoon sun was sinking in the west the little girl said she must be getting home, for her grandma would be anxious about her. The three bears would not let her go alone, so they all set off together through the twilight woods,—a merry company.

Golden Hair rode on the broad back of Papa Bear, while Mamma Bear and Tiny strode gaily on either side. In this way before night had fallen they came clear of the woods and up to the home of Golden Hair.

To be sure, the grandmother was much surprised to see this shaggy company with her little Golden Hair; but when she saw how jolly they all were and how handy they were in helping Golden Hair get the supper, she was delighted to have them stay, and gave them welcome. Papa Bear split the wood, brought it in, and built the fire. Mamma Bear got the tea kettle and filled it with water that was carried from the well by the Tiny Bear. And soon they were able to sit down to a good supper of hot biscuits, wild honey and pumpkin pie, with tea for the elders and nice sweet milk for Golden Hair and the Tiny Bear.

The grandmother liked the three bears so well and the bears were so delighted with the comforts of home that they all decided to live together for the general good.

Element Focus: Setting

In what ways did the setting make
the story more suspenseful?

Alice's Adventures in Wonderland

by Lewis Carroll

There was a table in front of the house. It was set out under a tree. The March Hare and the Hatter were having tea at it. A Dormouse was sitting between them. He was fast asleep. The other two were using it as a cushion. They were resting their elbows on it, and talking over its head. 'Very uncomfortable for the Dormouse,' thought Alice. 'Only, as it is asleep, I guess it doesn't mind.'

The table was a large one. But the three were all crowded together at one corner of it. 'No room! No room!' they cried out when they saw Alice coming. 'There's PLENTY of room!' said Alice. She sat down in a large arm chair at one end of the table.

'Have some wine,' the March Hare said.

Alice looked all round the table. But there was nothing on it but tea. 'I don't see any wine,' she said.

'There isn't any,' said the March Hare.

'Then it wasn't very nice of you to offer it,' said Alice angrily.

'It wasn't very nice of you to sit down without being invited,' said the March Hare.

'I didn't know it was YOUR table,' said Alice. 'It's set for many more than three.'

'Your hair needs to be cut,' said the Hatter. He had been looking at Alice for some time with great curiosity. But, this was the first time he spoke.

'You should learn not to make personal remarks,' Alice said. She sounded harsh. 'It's very rude.'

When he heard that, the Hatter opened his eyes very wide. But all he SAID was, 'Why is a raven like a writing desk?'

'We shall have some fun now!' thought Alice. 'I'm glad they have started to ask riddles.' Then she added aloud, 'I believe I can guess that.'

'Do you mean that you think you can find out the answer to it?' said the March Hare.

'Yes,' said Alice.

'Then you should say what you mean,' the March Hare said.

'I do,' Alice said quickly. 'Or, I mean what I say. That's the same thing.'

'No! That is not the same thing!' said the Hatter. 'You might just as well say that "I see what I eat" is the same thing as "I eat what I see!"'

'You might just as well say,' added the March Hare, 'that "I like what I get" is the same thing as "I get what I like!"'

The Dormouse seemed to be talking in his sleep. 'You might just as well say,' he said, 'that "I breathe when I sleep" is the same thing as "I sleep when I breathe!"'

'It IS the same thing with you,' said the Hatter. Here the conversation dropped. The party sat silent for a minute. Alice thought over all she could remember about ravens and writing desks. But, that wasn't much.

Element Focus: Character

How would you describe the conversation the characters had at this party? Is it what you would expect at a normal tea party? Explain.

Excerpt from

Alice's Adventures in Wonderland

by Lewis Carroll

There was a table set out under a tree in front of the house. The March Hare and the Hatter were having tea at it. A Dormouse was sitting between them, fast asleep. And the other two were using it as a cushion, resting their elbows on it, and talking over its head. 'Very uncomfortable for the Dormouse,' thought Alice. 'Only, as it's asleep, I suppose it doesn't mind.'

The table was a large one, but the three were all crowded together at one corner of it. 'No room! No room!' they cried out when they saw Alice coming. 'There's PLENTY of room!' said Alice indignantly. She sat down in a large arm chair at one end of the table.

'Have some wine,' the March Hare said.

Alice looked all round the table, but there was nothing on it but tea. 'I don't see any wine,' she remarked.

'There isn't any,' said the March Hare.

'Then it wasn't very polite of you to offer it,' said Alice angrily.

'It wasn't very polite of you to sit down without being invited,' said the March Hare.

'I didn't know it was YOUR table,' said Alice. 'It's set for a great many more than three.'

'Your hair needs to be cut,' said the Hatter. He had been looking at Alice for some time with great curiosity. But this was the first time he spoke.

'You should learn not to make personal remarks,' Alice said with some severity. 'It's very rude.'

The Hatter opened his eyes very wide on hearing this. But all he SAID was, 'Why is a raven like a writing desk?'

'Come, we shall have some fun now!' thought Alice. 'I'm glad they've begun asking riddles—I believe I can guess that,' she added aloud.

'Do you mean that you think you can find out the answer to it?' said the March Hare.

'Yes,' said Alice.

'Then you should say what you mean,' the March Hare went on.

'I do,' Alice said quickly. 'At least—at least I mean what I say. That's the same thing, you know.'

'Not the same thing a bit!' said the Hatter. 'You might just as well say that "I see what I eat" is the same thing as "I eat what I see!"'

'You might just as well say,' added the March Hare, 'that "I like what I get" is the same thing as "I get what I like!"'

'You might just as well say,' added the Dormouse, who seemed to be talking in his sleep, 'that "I breathe when I sleep" is the same thing as "I sleep when I breathe!"'

'It IS the same thing with you,' said the Hatter. Here the conversation dropped. The party sat silent for a minute. Alice thought over all she could remember about ravens and writing desks, which wasn't much.

Element Focus: Character

What if the characters at the tea party behaved the way you would expect people at a tea party to behave? How might their conversation be different?

Excerpt from

Alice's Adventures in Wonderland

by Lewis Carroll

There was a table set out under a tree in front of the house, and the March Hare and the Hatter were having tea at it: a Dormouse was sitting between them, fast asleep, and the other two were using it as a cushion, resting their elbows on it, and talking over its head. 'Very uncomfortable for the Dormouse,' thought Alice; 'only, as it's asleep, I suppose it doesn't mind.'

The table was a large one, but the three were all crowded together at one corner of it: 'No room! No room!' they cried out when they saw Alice coming. 'There's PLENTY of room!' said Alice indignantly, and she sat down in a large arm-chair at one end of the table.

'Have some wine,' the March Hare said in an encouraging tone. Alice looked all round the table, but there was nothing on it but tea. 'I don't see any wine,' she remarked.

'There isn't any,' said the March Hare.

'Then it wasn't very civil of you to offer it,' said Alice angrily.

'It wasn't very civil of you to sit down without being invited,' said the March Hare.

'I didn't know it was YOUR table,' said Alice; 'it's laid for a great many more than three.'

'Your hair wants cutting,' said the Hatter. He had been looking at Alice for some time with great curiosity, and this was his first speech.

'You should learn not to make personal remarks,' Alice said with some severity; 'it's very rude.'

The Hatter opened his eyes very wide on hearing this; but all he SAID was, 'Why is a raven like a writing-desk?'

'Come, we shall have some fun now!' thought Alice. 'I'm glad they've begun asking riddles.—I believe I can guess that,' she added aloud.

'Do you mean that you think you can find out the answer to it?' said the March Hare.

'Exactly so,' said Alice.

'Then you should say what you mean,' the March Hare went on.

'I do,' Alice hastily replied; 'at least—at least I mean what I say—that's the same thing, you know.'

'Not the same thing a bit!' said the Hatter. 'You might just as well say that "I see what I eat" is the same thing as "I eat what I see!"'

'You might just as well say,' added the March Hare, 'that "I like what I get" is the same thing as "I get what I like!"'

'You might just as well say,' added the Dormouse, who seemed to be talking in his sleep, 'that "I breathe when I sleep" is the same thing as "I sleep when I breathe!"'

'It IS the same thing with you,' said the Hatter, and here the conversation dropped, and the party sat silent for a minute, while Alice thought over all she could remember about ravens and writing-desks, which wasn't much.

Element Focus: Character

Describe several ways how the character dialogue in this text is different from what you might expect at a more traditional tea party.

Excerpt from

Alice's Adventures in Wonderland

by Lewis Carroll

As she approached, Alice could see that there was a table set out under a tree in front of the house, and the March Hare and the Hatter were having tea at it; a Dormouse was sitting between them, fast asleep, and the other two were using it as a cushion, resting their elbows on it, and talking over its head. 'That must be exceedingly uncomfortable for the Dormouse,' thought Alice, 'only, as it's asleep, I suppose it doesn't mind too much.'

The table was a large one, but the three were all crowded together at one corner of it. 'No room! No room!' they cried out when they noticed Alice coming. 'There's PLENTY of room!' declared Alice indignantly, and she plopped herself down in a large arm chair at one end of the table.

'Have some wine,' the March Hare said in an encouraging tone, so Alice scanned the table carefully, but she could discover nothing drinkable on it but tea. 'I don't see any wine,' she remarked.

'There isn't any,' revealed the March Hare.

'Then it wasn't very civil of you to offer it,' Alice intoned angrily.

'It wasn't very civil of you to sit down without being invited,' retorted the March Hare pointedly.

'I didn't know it was YOUR table,' observed Alice. 'It's laid for a great many more than three.'

'Your hair is certainly in need of cutting,' the Hatter stated matter-of-factly. He had been studiously regarding Alice for some time with great curiosity, and this was his first speech.

'You should learn not to make personal remarks,' Alice said with some apparent severity. 'It's extremely rude.'

The Hatter opened his eyes very wide indeed upon hearing this; but all he SAID was, 'Why is a raven like a writing desk?'

'Come, we shall have some fun now!' thought Alice with relief. 'I'm glad they've begun asking riddles—I believe I can guess that,' she added aloud.

'Do you mean that you think you can find out the answer to it?' demanded the March Hare.

'Exactly so,' stated Alice.

'Then you should say what you mean,' the March Hare continued.

'I do,' Alice hastily replied, 'at least—at least I mean what I say—that's the same thing, you know.'

'Not the same thing even a bit!' declared the Hatter emphatically. 'You might just as well declare that "I see what I eat" is the same thing as "I eat what I see!"'

'You might just as well declare,' added the March Hare, 'that "I like what I get" is the same thing as "I get what I like!"'

'You might just as well declare,' added the Dormouse, who seemed to be talking in his sleep, 'that "I breathe when I sleep" is the same thing as "I sleep when I breathe!"'

'It IS the same thing with you,' stated the Hatter, and here the conversation dropped, and the party sat silent for a minute, while Alice considered all she could remember about ravens and writing desks, which wasn't much.

Element Focus: Character

In what ways does the unexpected dialogue in the tea party differ from what one might expect at a typical tea party? How do these differences contribute to the humor of the scene?

Anne of Green Gables

by Lucy Maud Montgomery

"I'll settle Miss Anne when she comes home," said Marilla grimly. She was shaving up kindling. She used the carving knife with a bit more force than was necessary. Matthew had come in. He was waiting patiently for his tea in his corner. "She's roaming somewhere with Diana. They'll be writing stories. Or they'll be practicing dialogues or some silliness! And she isn't ever thinking once about the time. She isn't thinking of her duties. She must be pulled up short and sudden on this sort of thing. Anne has no business to leave the house like this! Not when I told her she was to stay home this afternoon and look after things. I must say she has many faults. But I never found her disobedient before. Nor has she been untrustworthy. I'm sorry she is now."

It was dark when supper was ready. There was still no sign of Anne. She was not hurrying over the log bridge. She was not running up Lover's Lane. She did not arrive breathless. She was not sorry about her neglected chores. Marilla washed up. She put away the dishes grimly. Then, she needed a candle to light her way down the cellar. So she went up to the east gable. She wanted the one that was on Anne's table. Lighting it, she turned around. There she saw Anne herself lying on the bed. She was face downward among the pillows.

"Mercy on us," said the surprised Marilla. "Have you been asleep, Anne?"

"No," said Anne.

"Are you sick?" Marilla asked, worried. She went over to the bed.

Anne hid deeper in her pillows. It was as if she wanted to hide forever from human eyes.

"No. But please, Marilla, go away. Don't look at me. I am deep in despair! I don't care who gets head in class. I don't care who writes the best composition. And I don't care who sings in the Sunday-school choir. Little things are not important now. I will not ever be able to go anywhere again. My career is closed. Please, Marilla, go away. And don't look at me."

"Did anyone ever hear the like?" Marilla wanted to know. "Anne Shirley, what is the matter with you? What have you done? Get right up this minute. Now, tell me. This minute, I say. There now, what is it?"

Anne had slid to the floor in sad obedience.

"Look at my hair," she whispered.

Marilla lifted her candle. She looked carefully at Anne's hair. It flowed in heavy masses down her back. It did have a very strange appearance.

"Anne Shirley, what have you done to your hair? Why, it's GREEN!"

Green it might be called, if it were any earthly color. It was a queer, dull, bronzy green. And there were streaks here and there of the original red. This just made it worse. Marilla had never seen anything so awful as Anne's hair at that moment.

"Yes, it's green," moaned Anne. "I thought nothing could be as bad as red hair. But now I know green hair is ten times worse. Oh, Marilla! You little know how utterly wretched I am."

"I little know how you got into this fix! But I mean to find out," said Marilla. "Come right down to the kitchen. It's too cold up here. Tell me just what you've done. I've been expecting something odd for some time. You have not got into any scrape for over two months. I was sure one was due. Now, then, what did you do to your hair?"

"I dyed it."

"Dyed it! Dyed your hair! Anne Shirley, didn't you know it was a wicked thing to do?"

Element Focus: Character

Why do you think Anne Shirley was
willing to risk dying her hair?

Excerpt from

Anne of Green Gables

by Lucy Maud Montgomery

"I'll settle Miss Anne when she comes home," said Marilla grimly. She was shaving up kindling. She used the carving knife with a bit more vim than was necessary. Matthew had come in. He was waiting patiently for his tea in his corner. "She's gadding off somewhere with Diana. They'll be writing stories or practicing dialogues or some such tomfoolery! And she isn't ever thinking once about the time or her duties. She's just got to be pulled up short and sudden on this sort of thing. Anne has no business to leave the house like this! Not when I told her she was to stay home this afternoon and look after things. I must say, with all her faults, I never found her disobedient or untrustworthy before. I'm real sorry to find her so now."

It was dark when supper was ready. There was still no sign of Anne, coming hurriedly over the log bridge or up Lover's Lane, breathless and repentant with a sense of neglected duties. Marilla washed and put away the dishes grimly. Then, she needed a candle to light her way down the cellar. So she went up to the east gable for the one that was on Anne's table. Lighting it, she turned around to see Anne herself lying on the bed. She was face downward among the pillows.

"Mercy on us," said astonished Marilla, "have you been asleep, Anne?"

"No," said Anne.

"Are you sick then?" demanded Marilla anxiously. She went over to the bed.

Anne cowered deeper into her pillows. It was as if she wanted to hide herself forever from mortal eyes.

"No. But please, Marilla, go away. Don't look at me. I'm in the depths of despair! I don't care who gets head in class. I don't care who writes the best composition. And I don't care who sings in the Sunday-school choir. Little things like that are of no importance now. I don't suppose I'll ever be able to go anywhere again. My career is closed. Please, Marilla, go away and don't look at me."

"Did anyone ever hear the like?" the mystified Marilla wanted to know. "Anne Shirley, whatever is the matter with you? What have you done? Get right up this minute and tell me. This minute, I say. There now, what is it?"

Anne had slid to the floor in sad obedience.

"Look at my hair, Marilla," she whispered.

Marilla lifted her candle and looked carefully at Anne's hair. It flowed in heavy masses down her back. It certainly had a very strange appearance.

"Anne Shirley, what have you done to your hair? Why, it's GREEN!"

Green it might be called, if it were any earthly color. It was a queer, dull, bronzy green. And there were streaks here and there of the original red to heighten the ghastly effect. Never in all her life had Marilla seen anything so grotesque as Anne's hair at that moment.

"Yes, it's green," moaned Anne. "I thought nothing could be as bad as red hair. But now I know it's ten times worse to have green hair. Oh, Marilla, you little know how utterly wretched I am."

"I little know how you got into this fix! But I mean to find out," said Marilla. "Come right down to the kitchen. It's too cold up here. Tell me just what you've done. I've been expecting something odd for some time. You haven't got into any scrape for over two months. I was sure another one was due. Now, then, what did you do to your hair?"

"I dyed it."

"Dyed it! Dyed your hair! Anne Shirley, didn't you know it was a wicked thing to do?"

Element Focus: Character

Are Marilla and Anne well-rounded or stereotypical characters? Explain several reasons for your answer.

Excerpt from

Anne of Green Gables

by Lucy Maud Montgomery

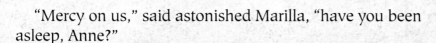

"I'll settle Miss Anne when she comes home," said Marilla grimly, as she shaved up kindlings with a carving knife and with more vim than was strictly necessary. Matthew had come in and was waiting patiently for his tea in his corner. "She's gadding off somewhere with Diana, writing stories or practicing dialogues or some such tomfoolery, and never thinking once about the time or her duties. She's just got to be pulled up short and sudden on this sort of thing. Anne has no business to leave the house like this when I told her she was to stay home this afternoon and look after things. I must say, with all her faults, I never found her disobedient or untrustworthy before and I'm real sorry to find her so now."

It was dark when supper was ready, and still no sign of Anne, coming hurriedly over the log bridge or up Lover's Lane, breathless and repentant with a sense of neglected duties. Marilla washed and put away the dishes grimly. Then, wanting a candle to light her way down the cellar, she went up to the east gable for the one that generally stood on Anne's table. Lighting it, she turned around to see Anne herself lying on the bed, face downward among the pillows.

"Mercy on us," said astonished Marilla, "have you been asleep, Anne?"

"No," was the muffled reply.

"Are you sick then?" demanded Marilla anxiously, going over to the bed.

Anne cowered deeper into her pillows as if desirous of hiding herself forever from mortal eyes.

"No. But please, Marilla, go away and don't look at me. I'm in the depths of despair and I don't care who gets head in class or writes the best composition or sings in the Sunday-school choir any more. Little things like that are of no importance now because I don't suppose I'll ever be able to go anywhere again. My career is closed. Please, Marilla, go away and don't look at me."

"Did anyone ever hear the like?" the mystified Marilla wanted to know. "Anne Shirley, whatever is the matter with you? What have you done? Get right up this minute and tell me. This minute, I say. There now, what is it?"

Anne had slid to the floor in despairing obedience.

"Look at my hair, Marilla," she whispered.

Accordingly, Marilla lifted her candle and looked scrutinizingly at Anne's hair, flowing in heavy masses down her back. It certainly had a very strange appearance.

"Anne Shirley, what have you done to your hair? Why, it's GREEN!"

Green it might be called, if it were any earthly color—a queer, dull, bronzy green, with streaks here and there of the original red to heighten the ghastly effect. Never in all her life had Marilla seen anything so grotesque as Anne's hair at that moment.

"Yes, it's green," moaned Anne. "I thought nothing could be as bad as red hair. But now I know it's ten times worse to have green hair. Oh, Marilla, you little know how utterly wretched I am."

"I little know how you got into this fix, but I mean to find out," said Marilla. "Come right down to the kitchen—it's too cold up here—and tell me just what you've done. I've been expecting something queer for some time. You haven't got into any scrape for over two months, and I was sure another one was due. Now, then, what did you do to your hair?"

"I dyed it."

"Dyed it! Dyed your hair! Anne Shirley, didn't you know it was a wicked thing to do?"

Element Focus: Character

Are Marilla and Anne well-rounded or stereotypical characters? How do their characteristics help to create the humor of the scene?

Anne of Green Gables

by Lucy Maud Montgomery

"I'll settle Miss Anne when she comes home," said Marilla grimly as she shaved up kindlings with a carving knife and with more vim than was strictly necessary. Matthew had come in and was waiting patiently for his tea in his corner. "She's gadding off somewhere with Diana, writing stories or practicing dialogues or some such tomfoolery, and never thinking once about the time or her duties. She's just got to be pulled up short and sudden on this sort of thing. Anne has no business to leave the house like this when I told her she was to stay home this afternoon and look after things. I must say, with all her faults, I never found her disobedient or untrustworthy before, and I'm real sorry to find her so now."

It was dark when supper was ready, and still no sign of Anne, coming hurriedly over the log bridge or up Lover's Lane, breathless and repentant with a sense of neglected duties. Marilla washed and put away the dishes grimly, then, wanting a candle to light her way down the cellar, she went up to the east gable for the one that generally stood on Anne's table. Lighting it, she turned around to see Anne herself lying on the bed, face downward among the pillows.

"Mercy upon us," cried astonished Marilla, "have you been asleep, Anne?"

"No," was the muffled reply from the pillows.

"Are you sick then?" demanded Marilla anxiously, going over to the bed.

Anne cowered deeper into her pillows as if desirous of hiding herself forever from mortal eyes.

"No, but please, Marilla, go away and don't look at me. I'm in the depths of despair, and I don't care who gets head in class or writes the best composition or sings in the Sunday-school choir any more. Little things like that are of no importance now because I don't suppose I'll ever be able to go anywhere again, so my career is closed. Please, Marilla, go away and don't look at me."

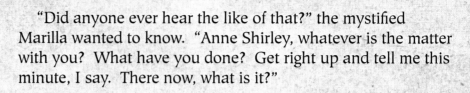

"Did anyone ever hear the like of that?" the mystified Marilla wanted to know. "Anne Shirley, whatever is the matter with you? What have you done? Get right up and tell me this minute, I say. There now, what is it?"

Anne had slid to the floor in despairing obedience.

"Look at my hair, Marilla," she whispered, her voice husky from tears.

Accordingly, Marilla lifted her candle and looked scrutinizingly at Anne's hair, flowing in heavy masses down her back. It certainly did have an exceedingly strange appearance.

"Anne Shirley, what have you done to your hair? Why, it's GREEN!"

Green it might be called, if it were any earthly color—a queer, dull, bronzy green, with streaks here and there of the original red to heighten the ghastly effect. Never in all her life had Marilla seen anything so grotesque as Anne's hair at that moment.

"Yes, it's green," moaned Anne. "I thought nothing could be as terrible as red hair, but now I know it's ten times worse to have green hair. Oh, Marilla, you little know how utterly wretched I am."

"I little know how you got into this fix, but I mean to find out," said Marilla. "Come right down to the kitchen—it's too cold up here—and tell me just what you've done. I've been expecting something queer for some time since you haven't gotten yourself into any scrape for over two months, and I was certain another one was due. Now, then, what did you do to your hair?"

"I dyed it," confessed Anne simply, too miserable to say more.

"Dyed it! Dyed your hair! Anne Shirley, didn't you realize it was a wicked thing to do?"

Element Focus: Character

Explain why you believe that Marilla and Anne are either well-rounded or stereotypical characters. How do their characteristics help to create the humor of the scene?

Excerpt from

The Magic Fishbone:
A Holiday Romance from the Pen of Miss Alice Rainbird

by Charles Dickens

Just then the old lady came jogging up. She was dressed in silk. It was of the richest quality. She smelled of dried lavender.

"King Watkins the First?" said the old lady.

"Watkins," said the king, "is my name."

"Papa of the beautiful Princess Alicia?" said the old lady.

"And of eighteen other darlings," said the king.

"Listen. You are going to the office," said the old lady.

Then the king knew that she must be a fairy. How could she know that?

"You are right," said the old lady. She answered his thoughts. "I am the Good Fairy Grandmarina. Listen. You will go home to dinner. Then politely invite the Princess Alicia to have some of the salmon you just bought."

"It may disagree with her," said the king.

The old lady became very angry. She knew this idea was absurd! She was so angry that the king was quite alarmed. He humbly begged her pardon.

"We hear a great deal too much about things disagreeing," said the old lady. Her voice showed she was disgusted. "Don't be greedy. I think you want it all."

The king hung his head. He said he wouldn't talk about things disagreeing any more.

"Be good, then," said the Fairy Grandmarina, "and don't! When the beautiful Princess Alicia eats the salmon—as I think she will—you will find she leaves a fish-bone on her plate. Tell her to dry it. Then she should rub it. And she should polish it till it shines like mother-of-pearl. Then tell her to take care of it. It is a present from me."

"Is that all?" asked the king.

"Don't be impatient," cried the fairy. She scolded him. "Don't catch people short! Don't speak before they have done speaking. Just the way with you grown-up persons. You are always doing it."

The king again hung his head. He said he would not do so any more.

"Be good then," said the Fairy Grandmarina, "and don't! Give the Princess Alicia my love. And tell her that the fish bone is a magic present. It can only be used once. It will bring her, that once, whatever she wishes for. But, she must wish for it at the right time. That is the message. Take care of it."

The king started, "Might I ask the reason—?" But, the fairy became furious.

"*Will* you be good, sir?" she cried. She stamped her foot. "The reason for this! And the reason for that, indeed! You are always wanting the reason. No reason. There! Hoity toity me! I am sick of your grown-up reasons."

The king was very frightened. He said he was very sorry to have offended her. He wouldn't ask for reasons any more.

Element Focus: Character

When Charles Dickens wrote this story, he pretended that a 7-year-old girl was telling it. How might you write the characters of the king and fairy differently if you were telling the tale?

The Magic Fishbone:
A Holiday Romance from the Pen of Miss Alice Rainbird

by Charles Dickens

Just then the old lady came trotting up. She was dressed in shot-silk. It was of the richest quality. And she smelled of dried lavender.

"King Watkins the First, I believe?" said the old lady.

"Watkins," agreed the king, "is my name."

"Papa, if I am not mistaken, of the beautiful Princess Alicia?" said the old lady.

"And of eighteen other darlings," said the king.

"Listen. You are going to the office," said the old lady.

Then the king knew that she must be a fairy. Or, how could she know that?

"You are right," said the old lady. She answered his thoughts. "I am the Good Fairy Grandmarina. Listen. When you go home to dinner, politely invite the Princess Alicia to have some of the salmon you just bought."

"It may disagree with her," said the king.

The old lady became very angry at this absurd idea! She was so angry that the king was quite alarmed. He humbly begged her pardon.

"We hear a great deal too much about things disagreeing," said the old lady. Her voice had the greatest contempt possible. "Don't be greedy. I think you want it all for you."

The king hung his head. He said he wouldn't talk about things disagreeing any more.

"Be good, then," said the Fairy Grandmarina, "and don't! When the beautiful Princess Alicia eats the salmon—as I think she will—you will find she will leave a fish-bone on her plate. Tell her to dry it. Then she should rub it and to polish it till it shines like mother-of-pearl. Then tell her to take care of it as a present from me."

"Is that all?" asked the king.

"Don't be impatient, sir," cried the Fairy Grandmarina. She was scolding him severely. "Don't catch people short! Don't speak before they have done speaking. Just the way with you grown-up persons. You are always doing it."

The king again hung his head. He said he wouldn't do so any more.

"Be good then," said the Fairy Grandmarina, "and don't! Tell the Princess Alicia, with my love, that the fish bone is a magic present. It can only be used once. But it will bring her, that once, whatever she wishes for. But, she must wish for it at the right time. That is the message. Take care of it."

The king began, "Might I ask the reason—?" But, the fairy became absolutely furious.

"*Will* you be good, sir?" she exclaimed. She stamped her foot on the ground. "The reason for this, and the reason for that, indeed! You are always wanting the reason. No reason. There! Hoity toity me! I am sick of your grown-up reasons."

The King was extremely frightened by the old lady's flying into such a passion, and said he was very sorry to have offended her, and he wouldn't ask for reasons any more.

Element Focus: Character

Charles Dickens wrote this story as if a bright 7-year-old girl was telling it. How does this affect the characters of the king and fairy?

The Magic Fishbone:
A Holiday Romance from the Pen of Miss Alice Rainbird

by Charles Dickens

Just then the old lady came trotting up. She was dressed in shot-silk of the richest quality, smelling of dried lavender.

"King Watkins the First, I believe?" said the old lady.

"Watkins," replied the King, "is my name."

"Papa, if I am not mistaken, of the beautiful Princess Alicia?" said the old lady.

"And of eighteen other darlings," replied the King.

"Listen. You are going to the office," said the old lady.

It instantly flashed upon the King that she must be a Fairy, or how could she know that?

"You are right," said the old lady, answering his thoughts, "I am the Good Fairy Grandmarina. Attend. When you return home to dinner, politely invite the Princess Alicia to have some of the salmon you bought just now."

"It may disagree with her," said the King.

The old lady became so very angry at this absurd idea, that the King was quite alarmed, and humbly begged her pardon.

"We hear a great deal too much about this thing disagreeing, and that thing disagreeing," said the old lady, with the greatest contempt it was possible to express. "Don't be greedy. I think you want it all yourself."

The King hung his head under this reproof, and said he wouldn't talk about things disagreeing, any more.

"Be good, then," said the Fairy Grandmarina, "and don't! When the beautiful Princess Alicia consents to partake of the salmon—as I think she will—you will find she will leave a fish-bone on her plate. Tell her to dry it, and to rub it, and to polish it till it shines like mother-of-pearl, and to take care of it as a present from me."

"Is that all?" asked the King.

"Don't be impatient, sir," returned the Fairy Grandmarina, scolding him severely. "Don't catch people short, before they have done speaking. Just the way with you grown-up persons. You are always doing it."

The King again hung his head, and said he wouldn't do so any more.

"Be good then," said the Fairy Grandmarina, "and don't! Tell the Princess Alicia, with my love, that the fish-bone is a magic present which can only be used once; but that it will bring her, that once, whatever she wishes for, provided she wishes for it at the right time. That is the message. Take care of it."

The King was beginning, "Might I ask the reason—?" when the Fairy became absolutely furious.

"*Will* you be good, sir?" she exclaimed, stamping her foot on the ground. "The reason for this, and the reason for that, indeed! You are always wanting the reason. No reason. There! Hoity toity me! I am sick of your grown-up reasons."

The King was extremely frightened by the old lady's flying into such a passion, and said he was very sorry to have offended her, and he wouldn't ask for reasons any more.

Element Focus: Character

Charles Dickens wrote this story as if a bright 7-year-old girl was telling it. Explain several ways that the characters of the King and Fairy might have been different if the author was supposed to be an adult.

The Magic Fishbone:
A Holiday Romance from the Pen of Miss Alice Rainbird

by Charles Dickens

Just then the old lady came trotting up. She was dressed in shot-silk of the richest quality, smelling of dried lavender.

"King Watkins the First, I believe?" inquired the old lady primly.

"Watkins," acknowledged the king, "is my name."

"Papa, if I am not mistaken, of the beautiful Princess Alicia?" pressed the old lady.

"And of eighteen other darlings," responded the king with some pride.

"Listen, you are going to the office," said the old lady matter-of-factly.

It instantly flashed upon the king that she must be a fairy, otherwise how could she know that?

"You are quite accurate," affirmed the old lady, answering his thoughts as if he had spoken them. "I am the Good Fairy Grandmarina. Attend carefully. When you return home to dinner, politely invite the Princess Alicia to have some of the salmon you bought just now."

"It may disagree with her," protested the king.

The old lady became so extremely furious at this absurd idea, that the king was quite alarmed, and found himself humbly begging her pardon.

"We hear a great deal too much about this thing disagreeing, and that thing disagreeing," said the enraged old lady, with the greatest contempt it was possible to express. "Don't be greedy, for I think the truth is that you want it all for yourself."

The king hung his head under this reproof, and said he wouldn't talk about things disagreeing, any more.

"Be a good man, then," admonished the Fairy Grandmarina, "and don't! When the beautiful Princess Alicia consents to partake of the salmon—as I think she will—you will find she will leave a fish-bone on her plate. Tell her to dry it, and to rub it, and to polish it till it shines like mother-of-pearl, and to take care of it as a present from me."

"Is that all?" asked the king a bit too hurriedly.

"Don't be impatient, sir," returned the Fairy Grandmarina, scolding him severely. "Don't catch people short, before they have done speaking. It is always the way with you grown-up persons. You are always doing it."

The king again hung his head, and said contritely that he wouldn't do so any more.

"Be a good man then," admonished the Fairy Grandmarina again, "and don't! Tell the Princess Alicia, with my love, that the fish bone is a magic present which can only be used once, but that it will bring her, that once, whatever she wishes for, provided she wishes for it at the right time. That is the message; be sure you take care of it."

The king was beginning, "Might I ask the reason—?" when the fairy became absolutely furious.

"*Will* you be good, sir?" she exclaimed, stamping her foot on the ground. "The reason for this, and the reason for that, indeed! You are always wanting the reason. There is no motive. There it is! Hoity toity me! I am completely sick of your grown-up reasons."

The king was extremely frightened by the old lady's flying into such a passion, and said he was very sorry to have offended her, and he wouldn't ask for reasons any more.

Element Focus: Character

Charles Dickens wrote this story as if a precocious 7-year-old girl was telling it. Describe several ways in which the characters of the king and fairy reveal the point of view of the pretend child author.

Excerpt from

The Book of Nature Myths:
Why the Bear Has a Short Tail

by Florence Holbrook

One cold morning the fox was coming up the road with some fish. There he met the bear.

"Good morning, Mr. Fox," said the bear.

"Good morning, Mr. Bear," said the fox. "The morning is brighter because I have met you."

"Those are very good fish, Mr. Fox," said the bear. "I have not eaten such fish for many a day. Where do you find them?"

"I have been fishing, Mr. Bear," answered the fox.

"If I could catch such fish as those, I should like to go fishing. But I do not know how to fish."

"It would be very easy for you to learn, Mr. Bear," said the fox. "You are so big and strong! You can do anything."

"Will you teach me, Mr. Fox?" asked the bear.

"I would not tell everybody. But you are such a good friend that I will teach you. Come to this pond. I will show you how to fish through the ice."

So the fox and the bear went to the frozen pond. The fox showed the bear how to make a hole in the ice.

"That is easy for you," said the fox. "But many an animal could not have made that hole. Now comes the secret. You must put your tail down into the water and keep it there. That is not easy, and not every animal could do it, for the water is very cold. But you are a learned animal, Mr. Bear. You know that the secret of catching fish is to keep your tail in the water a long time. Then when you pull it up, you will pull with it as many fish as I have."

The bear put his tail down into the water, and the fox went away. The sun rose high in the heavens, and still the bear sat with his tail through the hole in the ice. Sunset came, but still the bear sat with his tail through the hole in the ice. He thought, "When an animal is really learned, he will not fear a little cold."

It began to be dark, and the bear said, "Now I will pull the fish out of the water. How good they will be!" He pulled and pulled, but not a fish came out. Worse than that, not all of his tail came out, for the end of it was frozen fast to the ice.

He went slowly down the road, growling angrily, "I wish I could find that fox!" But the cunning fox was curled up in his warm nest. And whenever he thought of the bear, he laughed.

Element Focus: Character

How would the story be different if it were
told from the point of view of the fox?

Excerpt from

The Book of Nature Myths:
Why the Bear Has a Short Tail

by Florence Holbrook

One cold morning when the fox was coming up the road with some fish, he met the bear.

"Good morning, Mr. Fox," said the bear.

"Good morning, Mr. Bear," said the fox. "The morning is brighter because I have met you."

"Those are very good fish, Mr. Fox," said the bear. "I have not eaten such fish for many a day. Where do you find them?"

"I have been fishing, Mr. Bear," answered the fox.

"If I could catch such fish as those, I should like to go fishing. But I do not know how to fish."

"It would be very easy for you to learn, Mr. Bear," said the fox. "You are so big and strong that you can do anything."

"Will you teach me, Mr. Fox?" asked the bear.

"I would not tell everybody, but you are such a good friend that I will teach you. Come to this pond, and I will show you how to fish through the ice."

So the fox and the bear went to the frozen pond, and the fox showed the bear how to make a hole in the ice.

"That is easy for you," said the fox, "but many an animal could not have made that hole. Now comes the secret. You must put your tail down into the water and keep it there. That is not easy, and not every animal could do it, for the water is very cold; but you are a learned animal, Mr. Bear, and you know that the secret of catching fish is to keep your tail in the water a long time. Then when you pull it up, you will pull with it as many fish as I have."

The bear put his tail down into the water, and the fox went away. The sun rose high in the heavens, and still the bear sat with his tail through the hole in the ice. Sunset came, but still the bear sat with his tail through the hole in the ice, for he thought, "When an animal is really learned, he will not fear a little cold."

It began to be dark, and the bear said, "Now I will pull the fish out of the water. How good they will be!" He pulled and pulled, but not a fish came out. Worse than that, not all of his tail came out, for the end of it was frozen fast to the ice.

He went slowly down the road, growling angrily, "I wish I could find that fox"; but the cunning fox was curled up in his warm nest, and whenever he thought of the bear he laughed.

Element Focus: Character

What if the story were told from the point of view of the fox or the bear? Pick which retelling you think would be funnier and give three reasons why.

Excerpt from

The Book of Nature Myths:
Why the Bear Has a Short Tail

by Florence Holbrook

One frosty morning when the fox was traipsing up the road with some fish, he encountered the bear.

"Good morning, Mr. Fox," said the bear in polite greeting.

"Good morning, Mr. Bear," replied the fox equally pleasantly. "The morning is all the brighter because I have met you."

"Those are exceptionally delicious-looking fish, Mr. Fox," said the bear. "I have not had the opportunity to eat such fish for many a day. Where did you happen to find them?"

"I have been fishing, Mr. Bear," answered the fox.

"If I could catch such fish as those, I should like to go fishing, but I do not know how to fish."

"It would be very easy for someone as impressive as you to learn, Mr. Bear," said the fox, the flattery dripping from his words like water from the damp fish. "You are so big and strong that you can do anything."

"Will you be so kind as to teach me, Mr. Fox?" asked the bear.

"I would not tell just anybody, but you are such a good friend that I will teach you. Come to this pond, and I will show you how to fish through the ice."

So the fox and the bear went to the frozen pond, and the fox showed the bear how to make a hole in the ice.

"See now, this is precisely what I meant before—that is easy for you," said the fox, "but many an animal could not have made that hole. Now comes the secret part: you must put your tail down into the water and keep it there. That is not easy, and not every animal could do it, for the water is extremely cold. But you are a learned animal, Mr. Bear. You are wise enough to understand that a little discomfort now can lead to great satisfaction later. You now know that the secret of catching fish is to keep your tail in the water a long time, so then when you pull it up, you will pull with it as many fish as I have."

The bear put his tail down into the water, and the fox went away. The sun rose high in the heavens, and still the bear sat with his tail through the hole in the ice. Sunset came, but still the bear sat with his tail through the hole in the ice, for he thought, "When an animal is really learned, he will not fear a little cold."

It began to be dark, and the bear said, "Now I will pull the fish out of the water. How good they will be!" He pulled and pulled, but not a fish came out. Worse than that, not all of his tail came out, for the end of it was frozen fast to the ice.

He went slowly down the road, growling angrily, "I wish I could find that fox"; but the cunning fox was curled up in his warm nest, and whenever he thought of the bear, he laughed.

Element Focus: Character

What if this story were told from the first person perspective of the fox? Would this make the story funnier or less funny?

Excerpt from

The Book of Nature Myths:
Why the Bear Has a Short Tail

by Florence Holbrook

One frosty morning when the fox was traipsing up the road with some fish, he encountered the bear.

"Good morning, Mr. Fox," said the bear in polite greeting.

"Good morning, Mr. Bear," replied the fox equally pleasantly. "The morning is all the brighter because I have met you."

"Those are exceptionally delicious-looking fish, Mr. Fox," said the bear. "I have not had the opportunity to eat such fish for many a day. Where did you happen to find them?"

"I have been fishing, Mr. Bear," answered the fox.

"If I could catch such fish as those, I should like to go fishing, but I do not know how to fish."

"It would be very easy for someone as impressive as you to learn, Mr. Bear," said the fox, the flattery dripping from his words like water from the damp fish. "You are so big and strong that you can do anything."

"Will you be so kind as to teach me, Mr. Fox?" asked the bear.

"I would not tell just anybody, but you are such a good friend that I will teach you. Come to this pond, and I will show you how to fish through the ice."

So the fox and the bear went to the frozen pond, and the fox showed the bear how to make a hole in the ice.

"See now, this is precisely what I meant before—that is easy for you," said the fox, "but many an animal could not have made that hole. Now comes the secret part: you must put your tail down into the water and keep it there. That is not easy, and not every animal could do it, for the water is extremely cold. But you are a learned animal, Mr. Bear. You are wise enough to understand that a little discomfort now can lead to great satisfaction later. You now know that the secret of catching fish is to keep your tail in the water a long time, so then when you pull it up, you will pull with it as many fish as I have."

The bear lowered his tail carefully into the water, and the fox padded away into the woods. The sun rose high in the heavens, but the bear continued to patiently sit with his tail thrust through the hole in the ice. Sunset came, but still the bear did not budge and stubbornly kept his tail lowered through the hole in the ice, for he thought, "When an animal is truly learned, he will not allow a little cold to get in the way of his goals."

Twilight came and the sky grew dark and the bear said to himself, "Now I will finally pull the fish out of the water. How good they will be after all this time!" He pulled and pulled, but not a single fish came out from the water, and worse than that, not all of his tail came out either, for the end of it was frozen fast to the ice.

Hungry, cold, and humiliated, he walked slowly down the road, growling angrily, "I wish I could find that rascal fox!" But the cunning fox was curled up in his warm nest with a full belly, chuckling happily to himself over the trick he had played on the gullible bear.

Element Focus: Character

What if this story were told from the first person perspective of the fox instead of the third person perspective of a narrator? How would this affect the humor level of the story?

Excerpt from
The Bremen Town Musicians

by The Brothers Grimm

Bremen was too far off to reach in one day. At evening they came to a wood. There they decided to pass the night. The donkey and the dog lay down under a large tree. The cat got up among the branches. And the rooster flew up to the top, as that was the safest place for him. Before he went to sleep, he looked all round him to the four points of the compass. In the distance he saw a little light shining. He called out to his friends that there must be a house not far off, as he could see a light. So the donkey said, "We had better get up and go there. This is not a comfortable spot." The dog began to think a few bones, not quite bare, would do him good. And they all set off in the direction of the light. It grew larger and brighter. At last it led them to a robber's house, all lighted up. The donkey was the biggest. So, he went up to the window and looked in.

"Well, what do you see?" asked the dog.

"What do I see?" answered the donkey. "Here is a table set out with splendid food and drinks. There are robbers sitting at it and making themselves very comfortable."

"That would just suit us," said the rooster.

"Yes, indeed. I wish we were there," said the donkey. Then they talked together about how to get the robbers out of the house. At last they hit on a plan. The donkey was to place his forefeet on the windowsill. The dog was to get on the donkey's back. The cat would climb on the top of the dog. And lastly, the rooster was to fly up and perch on the cat's head. When that was done, at a given signal, they all began to perform their music. The donkey brayed. The dog barked. The cat mewed. And the rooster crowed. Then they burst through into the room, breaking all the panes of glass. The robbers fled at the dreadful sound! They thought it was some goblin! So, they ran to the wood in terror. Then the four friends sat down to table and enjoyed what was left of the meal. They feasted as if they had been hungry for a month.

And when they had finished, they put out the lights. Each found a sleeping place to suit his nature and habits. The donkey laid himself down outside on the dunghill. The dog curled up behind the door. The cat sat on the hearth by the warm ashes. And the rooster roosted in the cockloft. They were all tired with their long trip. So, they soon fell fast asleep.

Around midnight, the robbers from afar saw that no light was burning. Everything looked quiet. So, their captain said to them that he thought that they had fled for no reason. He ordered one of them to go check. So, one of them went. He found everything quite quiet. He went into the kitchen to strike a light. But, he made a mistake. He thought the glowing, fiery eyes of the cat were burning coals! He held a match to them in order to light it. But the cat did not see this as a joke! It flew into his face, spitting and scratching. Then he cried out in terror! He ran to get out at the back door! But the dog, who was lying there, ran at him and bit his leg. As he was rushing through the yard by the dunghill, the donkey struck out and gave him a great kick with his hind foot. The rooster had been wakened with the noise! Feeling excited, he cried out, "Cock-a-doodle-doo!"

Then the robber got back as well as he could to his captain. He said, "Oh dear! In that house there is a gruesome witch! I felt her breath and her long nails in my face. By the door there stands a man who stabbed me in the leg with a knife. And in the yard there lies a black spirit who beat me with his wooden club. Above, upon the roof, there sits the justice! He cried, 'Bring that rogue here!' And so, I ran away from the place as fast as I could."

From that time forward, the robbers never dared to go to that house. The four Bremen town musicians found themselves well off where they were, though. So, there they stayed. And the person who last related this tale is still living, as you see.

Element Focus: Plot

The climax is the most exciting part of the story. Which part of this story is the climax? Support your reason for thinking it is more exciting than the rest.

The Bremen Town Musicians

by The Brothers Grimm

Bremen was too far off to reach in one day. At evening they came to a wood. There they decided to pass the night. The donkey and the dog lay down under a large tree. The cat got up among the branches. And the rooster flew up to the top, as that was the safest place for him. Before he went to sleep, he looked all round him to the four points of the compass. In the distance he saw a little light shining. He called out to his friends that there must be a house not far off, as he could see a light. So the donkey said, "We had better get up and go there. This is not a comfortable spot." The dog began to think a few bones, not quite bare, would do him good. And they all set off in the direction of the light. It grew larger and brighter. At last it led them to a robber's house, all lighted up. The donkey was the biggest. So, he went up to the window and looked in.

"Well, what do you see?" asked the dog.

"What do I see?" answered the donkey. "Here is a table set out with splendid food and drinks. There are robbers sitting at it and making themselves very comfortable."

"That would just suit us," said the rooster.

"Yes, indeed. I wish we were there," said the donkey. Then they talked together about how to get the robbers out of the house. At last they hit on a plan. The donkey was to place his forefeet on the windowsill. The dog was to get on the donkey's back. The cat would climb on the top of the dog. And lastly, the rooster was to fly up and perch on the cat's head. When that was done, at a given signal, they all began to perform their music. The donkey brayed, the dog barked, the cat mewed, and the rooster crowed. Then they burst through into the room, breaking all the panes of glass. The robbers fled at the dreadful sound! They thought it was some goblin, and ran to the wood in the utmost terror. Then the four companions sat down to table and made free with the remains of the meal. They feasted as if they had been hungry for a month.

And when they had finished, they put out the lights. Each sought out a sleeping place to suit his nature and habits. The donkey laid himself down outside on the dunghill. The dog curled up behind the door. The cat settled on the hearth by the warm ashes. And the rooster roosted in the cockloft. As they were all tired with their long journey, they soon fell fast asleep.

When midnight drew near, the robbers from afar saw that no light was burning. Everything appeared quiet, so their captain said to them that he thought that they had run away without reason. He ordered one of them to go investigate. So one of them went, and found everything quite quiet. He went into the kitchen to strike a light, and taking the glowing, fiery eyes of the cat for burning coals, he held a match to them in order to kindle it. But the cat, not seeing the joke, flew into his face, spitting and scratching. Then he cried out in terror, and ran to get out at the back door! But the dog, who was lying there, ran at him and bit his leg. As he was rushing through the yard by the dunghill, the donkey struck out and gave him a great kick with his hind foot. And the rooster, who had been wakened with the noise, and felt quite brisk, cried out, "Cock-a-doodle-doo!"

Then the robber got back as well as he could to his captain. He said, "Oh dear! In that house there is a gruesome witch, and I felt her breath and her long nails in my face. By the door there stands a man who stabbed me in the leg with a knife. And in the yard there lies a black spectre, who beat me with his wooden club. Above, upon the roof, there sits the justice, who cried, 'Bring that rogue here!' And so, I ran away from the place as fast as I could."

From that time forward, the robbers never ventured to that house. The four Bremen town musicians found themselves so well off where they were, that there they stayed. And the person who last related this tale is still living, as you see.

Element Focus: Plot

The climax is the most exciting part of the story.
Which paragraph is the climax of this story?
Explain several reasons why you chose it.

Excerpt from

The Bremen Town Musicians

by The Brothers Grimm

Bremen was too far off to be reached in one day. Towards evening they came to a wood where they decided to pass the night. The donkey and the dog lay down under a large tree. The cat got up among the branches. And the rooster flew up to the top, as that was the safest place for him. Before he went to sleep, he looked all round him to the four points of the compass. In the distance he saw a little light shining. He called out to his companions that there must be a house not far off, as he could see a light. So the donkey said, "We had better get up and go there, for these are uncomfortable quarters." The dog began to fancy a few bones, not quite bare, would do him good. And they all set off in the direction of the light. It grew larger and brighter, until at last it led them to a robber's house, all lighted up. The donkey, being the biggest, went up to the window, and looked in.

"Well, what do you see?" asked the dog.

"What do I see?" answered the donkey. "Here is a table set out with splendid eatables and drinkables, and robbers sitting at it and making themselves very comfortable."

"That would just suit us," said the rooster.

"Yes, indeed, I wish we were there," said the donkey. Then they consulted together how it should be managed so as to get the robbers out of the house, and at last they hit on a plan. The donkey was to place his forefeet on the windowsill, the dog was to get on the donkey's back, the cat on the top of the dog, and lastly the rooster was to fly up and perch on the cat's head. When that was done, at a given signal they all began to perform their music. The donkey brayed, the dog barked, the cat mewed, and the rooster crowed. Then they burst through into the room, breaking all the panes of glass. The robbers fled at the dreadful sound! They thought it was some goblin, and ran to the wood in the utmost terror. Then the four companions sat down to table and made free with the remains of the meal. They feasted as if they had been hungry for a month.

And when they had finished they put out the lights. Each sought out a sleeping-place to suit his nature and habits. The donkey laid himself down outside on the dunghill, the dog behind the door, the cat on the hearth by the warm ashes, and the rooster settled himself in the cockloft, and as they were all tired with their long journey, they soon fell fast asleep.

When midnight drew near, and the robbers from afar saw that no light was burning, and that everything appeared quiet, their captain said to them that he thought that they had run away without reason, telling one of them to go and reconnoitre. So one of them went, and found everything quite quiet; he went into the kitchen to strike a light, and taking the glowing, fiery eyes of the cat for burning coals, he held a match to them in order to kindle it. But the cat, not seeing the joke, flew into his face, spitting and scratching. Then he cried out in terror, and ran to get out at the back door, but the dog, who was lying there, ran at him and bit his leg; and as he was rushing through the yard by the dunghill, the donkey struck out and gave him a great kick with his hind foot; and the rooster, who had been wakened with the noise, and felt quite brisk, cried out, "Cock-a-doodle-doo!"

Then the robber got back as well as he could to his captain, and said, "Oh dear! In that house there is a gruesome witch, and I felt her breath and her long nails in my face; and by the door there stands a man who stabbed me in the leg with a knife; and in the yard there lies a black spectre, who beat me with his wooden club; and above, upon the roof, there sits the justice, who cried, 'Bring that rogue here!' And so, I ran away from the place as fast as I could."

From that time forward the robbers never ventured to that house, and the four Bremen town musicians found themselves so well off where they were, that there they stayed. And the person who last related this tale is still living, as you see.

Element Focus: Plot

Explain several reasons why the climax of this story is more exciting than the rest of it.

The Bremen Town Musicians

by The Brothers Grimm

Bremen was too far off to be reached in one day, and towards evening they came to a wood, where they determined to pass the night. The donkey and the dog lay down under a large tree; the cat got up among the branches, and the rooster flew up to the top, as that was the safest place for him. Before he went to sleep he looked all round him to the four points of the compass, and perceived in the distance a little light shining, and he called out to his companions that there must be a house not far off, as he could see a light, so the donkey said, "We had better get up and go there, for these are uncomfortable quarters." The dog began to fancy a few bones, not quite bare, would do him good. And they all set off in the direction of the light, and it grew larger and brighter, until at last it led them to a robber's house, all lighted up. The donkey, being the biggest, went up to the window, and looked in.

"Well, what do you see?" asked the dog.

"What do I see?" answered the donkey; "here is a table set out with splendid eatables and drinkables, and robbers sitting at it and making themselves very comfortable."

"That would just suit us," said the rooster.

"Yes, indeed, I wish we were there," said the donkey. Then they consulted together how it should be managed so as to get the robbers out of the house, and at last they hit on a plan. The donkey was to place his forefeet on the windowsill, the dog was to get on the donkey's back, the cat on the top of the dog, and lastly the rooster was to fly up and perch on the cat's head. When that was done, at a given signal they all began to perform their music. The donkey brayed, the dog barked, the cat mewed, and the rooster crowed; then they burst through into the room, breaking all the panes of glass. The robbers fled at the dreadful sound; they thought it was some goblin, and fled to the wood in the utmost terror. Then the four companions sat down to table, made free with the remains of the meal, and feasted as if they had been hungry for a month.

And when they had finished they put out the lights, and each sought out a sleeping place to suit his nature and habits. The donkey laid himself down outside on the dunghill, the dog behind the door, the cat on the hearth by the warm ashes, and the rooster settled himself in the cockloft, and as they were all tired with their long journey they soon fell fast asleep.

When midnight drew near, and the robbers from afar saw that no light was burning, and that everything appeared quiet, their captain said to them that he thought that they had run away without reason, telling one of them to go and reconnoitre. So one of them went, and found everything quite quiet; he went into the kitchen to strike a light, and taking the glowing fiery eyes of the cat for burning coals, he held a match to them in order to kindle it. But the cat, not seeing the joke, flew into his face, spitting and scratching. Then he cried out in terror, and ran to get out at the back door, but the dog, who was lying there, ran at him and bit his leg; and as he was rushing through the yard by the dunghill the donkey struck out and gave him a great kick with his hind foot; and the rooster, who had been wakened with the noise, and felt quite brisk, cried out, "Cock-a-doodle-doo!"

Then the robber got back as well as he could to his captain, and said, "Oh dear! In that house there is a grewsome witch, and I felt her breath and her long nails in my face; and by the door there stands a man who stabbed me in the leg with a knife; and in the yard there lies a black spectre, who beat me with his wooden club; and above, upon the roof, there sits the justice, who cried, 'Bring that rogue here!' And so I ran away from the place as fast as I could."

From that time forward the robbers never ventured to that house, and the four Bremen town musicians found themselves so well off where they were, that there they stayed. And the person who last related this tale is still living, as you see.

Element Focus: Plot

Describe several ways that the authors created excitement in the climax of the story.

Clever Else

by The Brothers Grimm

There was once a man who had a daughter. She was called "Clever Else." When she was grown up, her father said she must be married. Her mother said, "Yes, if we could only find someone that she would agree to have."

At last one came from a distance. His name was Hans. He proposed to her. But he made it a condition that Clever Else should be very careful, too.

They were all seated at the table. They had eaten well. So, the mother said, "Else, go into the cellar and get some beer."

Then Clever Else took down the jug from the hook in the wall. She rattled the lid up and down so as to pass away the time on the way to the cellar. When she got there, she took a stool and stood it in front of the cask. This was so that she need not stoop and make her back ache. Then she put the jug under the tap. And she turned it. While the beer was running, she did not want her eyes to be idle. So she glanced here and there. Finally, she noticed a pickaxe that the workmen had left sticking in the ceiling. It was just above her head. Then Clever Else began to cry. She thought, "What if I marry Hans, and we have a child, and it grows big? And what if we send it into the cellar to get beer? That pickaxe might fall on his head and kill him."

So there she sat and cried with all her might. She was mourning over the evil that might come in the future. All the while they were waiting upstairs for something to drink. They waited and waited. At last the mistress turned to the maid. "Go down and see why Else does not come."

So the maid went. She found Else sitting in front of the cask. She was crying with all her might.

"What are you crying for?" said the maid.

"Oh dear me!" answered she. "How can I help crying? If I marry Hans, and we have a child, and it grows big, we may send it here to draw beer. Then maybe the pickaxe will fall on its head and kill it."

"Our Else is clever indeed!" said the maid, and sat down to weep for the future misfortune. After a while, the people upstairs found that the maid did not return. They were becoming more and more thirsty. So the master said to the boy, "You go down into the cellar. See what Else and the maid are doing."

The boy did so. There he found both Clever Else and the maid sitting crying together. Then he asked what was the matter.

"Oh dear me," said Else, "how can we help crying? If I marry Hans, we may have a child that grows big. If we send it here to draw beer, the pickaxe might fall on its head and kill it."

"Our Else is clever indeed!" said the boy. Then sitting down beside her, he began howling with a good will. Upstairs they were all waiting for him to come back. But he did not come. So the master said to the mistress, "You go down to the cellar and see what Else is doing."

So the mistress went down. She found all three in great distress. She asked the cause. So Else told her how the future possible child might be killed as soon as it was big enough to be sent to draw beer, by the pickaxe falling on it. Then the mother at once exclaimed, "Our Else is clever indeed!" And, sitting down, she wept with the rest.

Upstairs the husband waited a little while. But his wife did not return. And his thirst got worse. So, he said, "I must go down to the cellar myself. I will see what has become of Else." And then he came into the cellar. There he found them all. They were sitting and weeping together. He was told that it was all owing to the child that Else might possibly have, and the possibility of its being killed by the pickaxe so happening to fall just at the time the child might be sitting underneath it drawing beer. All this he heard. And he cried, "How clever is our Else!" Then he sat down. And he joined his tears to theirs.

The intended bridegroom stayed upstairs. He was by himself a long time. But nobody came back to him. So, he thought he would go himself and see what they were all about. And there he found all five moaning and crying most pitifully. Each one was louder than the other.

"What misfortune has happened?" cried he.

"O my dear Hans," said Else, "if we marry and have a child, and it grows big, we may send it down here to get beer! Perhaps that pickaxe which has been left sticking up there might fall down on the child's head and kill it! How can we help crying at that?"

"Now," said Hans, "I cannot think that greater sense than that could be wanted in my household. You are so clever, Else! I will have you for my wife." And taking her by the hand, he led her upstairs. They had the wedding at once.

Element Focus: Plot

Propose a solution for Clever Else's problem.

#50988—*Leveled Texts for Classic Fiction: Humor*
© *Shell Education*

Excerpt from

Clever Else

by The Brothers Grimm

There was once a man who had a daughter called "Clever Else." When she was grown up, her father said she must be married. Her mother said, "Yes, if we could only find someone that she would agree to have."

At last one came from a distance. His name was Hans. When he proposed to her, he made it a condition that Clever Else should be very careful, too.

They were all seated at the table, and had well eaten. So, the mother said, "Else, go into the cellar and draw some beer."

Then Clever Else took down the jug from the hook in the wall. She rattled the lid up and down so as to pass away the time on the way to the cellar. When she got there, she took a stool and stood it in front of the cask. This was so that she need not stoop and make her back ache. Then she put the jug under the tap. And she turned it. While the beer was running, she did not want her eyes to be idle. So she glanced here and there. Finally, she noticed a pickaxe that the workmen had left sticking in the ceiling. It was just above her head. Then Clever Else began to cry. She thought, "What if I marry Hans, and we have a child, and it grows big? And what if we send it into the cellar to draw beer? That pickaxe might fall on his head and kill him."

So there she sat and cried with all her might. She was mourning over the evil that might come in the future. All the while they were waiting upstairs for something to drink. They waited in vain. At last the mistress turned to the maid. "Go down to the cellar and see why Else does not come."

So the maid went. And she found Else sitting in front of the cask. She was crying with all her might.

"What are you crying for?" said the maid.

"Oh dear me!" answered she. "How can I help crying? If I marry Hans, and we have a child, and it grows big, we may send it here to draw beer. Then perhaps the pickaxe will fall on its head and kill it."

"Our Else is clever indeed!" said the maid, and directly sat down to bewail the anticipated misfortune. After a while, the people upstairs found that the maid did not return. They were becoming more and more thirsty, so the master said to the boy, "You go down into the cellar. See what Else and the maid are doing."

The boy did so. There he found both Clever Else and the maid sitting crying together. Then he asked what was the matter.

"Oh dear me," said Else, "how can we help crying? If I marry Hans, and we have a child, and it grows big, and we send it here to draw beer, the pickaxe might fall on its head and kill it."

"Our Else is clever indeed!" said the boy. Then sitting down beside her, he began howling with a good will. Upstairs they were all waiting for him to come back. But as he did not come, the master said to the mistress, "You go down to the cellar and see what Else is doing."

So the mistress went down and found all three in great distress. When she asked the cause, Else told her how the future possible child might be killed as soon as it was big enough to be sent to draw beer, by the pickaxe falling on it. Then the mother at once exclaimed, "Our Else is clever indeed!" And, sitting down, she wept with the rest.

Upstairs the husband waited a little while. But as his wife did not return, and as his thirst constantly increased, he said, "I must go down to the cellar myself. I will see what has become of Else." And then he came into the cellar. There he found them all sitting and weeping together. He was told that it was all owing to the child that Else might possibly have, and the possibility of its being killed by the pickaxe so happening to fall just at the time the child might be sitting underneath it drawing beer. And when he heard all this, he cried, "How clever is our Else!" and sitting down, he joined his tears to theirs.

The intended bridegroom stayed upstairs by himself a long time. But as nobody came back to him, he thought he would go himself and see what they were all about. And there he found all five lamenting and crying most pitifully. Each one was louder than the other.

"What misfortune has happened?" cried he.

"O my dear Hans," said Else, "if we marry and have a child, and it grows big, and we send it down here to draw beer, perhaps that pickaxe which has been left sticking up there might fall down on the child's head and kill it! How can we help crying at that?"

"Now," said Hans, "I cannot think that greater sense than that could be wanted in my household. So as you are so clever, Else, I will have you for my wife." And taking her by the hand, he led her upstairs. They had the wedding at once.

Element Focus: Plot

What sequel could result from this story?

Clever Else

by The Brothers Grimm

There was once a man who had a daughter who was called "Clever Else." When she was grown up, her father said she must be married. Her mother said, "Yes, if we could only find someone that she would consent to have."

At last one came from a distance. His name was Hans, and when he proposed to her, he made it a condition that Clever Else should be very careful, too.

Now when they were all seated at the table, and had well eaten, the mother said, "Else, go into the cellar and draw some beer."

Then Clever Else took down the jug from the hook in the wall. As she was on her way to the cellar, she rattled the lid up and down so as to pass away the time. When she got there, she took a stool and stood it in front of the cask. This was so that she need not stoop and make her back ache with needless trouble. Then she put the jug under the tap and turned it. While the beer was running, in order that her eyes should not be idle, she glanced hither and thither. Finally, she caught sight of a pickaxe that the workmen had left sticking in the ceiling just above her head. Then Clever Else began to cry, for she thought, "If I marry Hans, and we have a child, and it grows big, and we send it into the cellar to draw beer, that pickaxe might fall on his head and kill him."

So there she sat and cried with all her might, lamenting the anticipated misfortune. All the while they were waiting upstairs for something to drink. They waited in vain. At last the mistress said to the maid, "Go down to the cellar and see why Else does not come."

So the maid went. And she found her sitting in front of the cask crying with all her might.

"What are you crying for?" said the maid.

"Oh dear me," answered she, "how can I help crying? If I marry Hans, and we have a child, and it grows big, and we send it here to draw beer, perhaps the pickaxe may fall on its head and kill it."

"Our Else is clever indeed!" said the maid, and directly sat down to bewail the anticipated misfortune. After a while, when the people upstairs found that the maid did not return, and they were becoming more and more thirsty. The master said to the boy, "You go down into the cellar. See what Else and the maid are doing."

The boy did so, and there he found both Clever Else and the maid sitting crying together. Then he asked what was the matter.

"Oh dear me," said Else, "how can we help crying? If I marry Hans, and we have a child, and it grows big, and we send it here to draw beer, the pickaxe might fall on its head and kill it."

"Our Else is clever indeed!" said the boy, and sitting down beside her, he began howling with a good will. Upstairs they were all waiting for him to come back, but he did not come. The master said to the mistress, "You go down to the cellar and see what Else is doing."

So the mistress went down and found all three in great cries. When she asked the cause, Else told her how the future possible child might be killed as soon as it was big enough to be sent to draw beer, by the pickaxe falling on it. Then the mother at once exclaimed, "Our Else is clever indeed!" And, sitting down, she wept with the rest.

Upstairs the husband waited a little while, but as his wife did not return, and as his thirst constantly increased, he said, "I must go down to the cellar myself, and see what has become of Else." And when he came into the cellar, and found them all sitting and weeping together, he was told that it was all owing to the child that Else might possibly have, and the possibility of its being killed by the pickaxe so happening to fall just at the time the child might be sitting underneath it drawing beer; and when he heard all this, he cried, "How clever is our Else!" and sitting down, he joined his tears to theirs.

The intended bridegroom stayed upstairs by himself a long time, but as nobody came back to him, he thought he would go himself and see what they were all about. And there he found all five lamenting and crying most pitifully. Each one louder than the other.

"What misfortune has happened?" cried he.

"O my dear Hans," said Else, "if we marry and have a child, and it grows big, and we send it down here to draw beer, perhaps that pickaxe which has been left sticking up there might fall down on the child's head and kill it. How can we help crying at that!"

"Now," said Hans, "I cannot think that greater sense than that could be wanted in my household. You are so clever, Else, I will have you for my wife," and taking her by the hand, he led her upstairs. They had the wedding at once.

Element Focus: Plot

What sequel could result from this story?

Excerpt from

Clever Else

by The Brothers Grimm

There was once a man who had a daughter who was called "Clever Else," and when she was grown up, her father said she must be married, and her mother said, "Yes, if we could only find someone that she would consent to have."

At last one came from a distance, and his name was Hans, and when he proposed to her, he made it a condition that Clever Else should be very careful as well.

Now when they were all seated at the table, and had well eaten, the mother said, "Else, go into the cellar and draw some beer."

Then Clever Else took down the jug from the hook in the wall, and as she was on her way to the cellar she rattled the lid up and down so as to pass away the time. When she got there, she took a stool and stood it in front of the cask, so that she need not stoop and make her back ache with needless trouble. Then she put the jug under the tap and turned it, and while the beer was running, in order that her eyes should not be idle, she glanced hither and thither, and finally caught sight of a pickaxe that the workmen had left sticking in the ceiling just above her head. Then Clever Else began to cry, for she thought, "If I marry Hans, and we have a child, and it grows big, and we send it into the cellar to draw beer, that pickaxe might fall on his head and kill him."

So there she sat and cried with all her might, lamenting the anticipated misfortune. All the while they were waiting upstairs for something to drink, and they waited in vain. At last the mistress said to the maid, "Go down to the cellar and see why Else does not come."

So the maid went, and found her sitting in front of the cask crying with all her might.

"What are you crying for?" said the maid.

"Oh dear me," answered she, "how can I help crying? If I marry Hans, and we have a child, and it grows big, and we send it here to draw beer, perhaps the pickaxe may fall on its head and kill it."

"Our Else is clever indeed!" said the maid, and directly sat down to bewail the anticipated misfortune. After a while, when the people upstairs found that the maid did not return, and they were becoming more and more thirsty, the master said to the boy, "You go down into the cellar, and see what Else and the maid are doing."

The boy did so, and there he found both Clever Else and the maid sitting crying together. Then he asked what was the matter.

"Oh dear me," said Else, "how can we help crying? If I marry Hans, and we have a child, and it grows big, and we send it here to draw beer, the pickaxe might fall on its head and kill it."

"Our Else is clever indeed!" said the boy, and sitting down beside her, he began howling with a good will. Upstairs they were all waiting for him to come back, but as he did not come, the master said to the mistress, "You go down to the cellar and see what Else is doing."

So the mistress went down and found all three in great lamentations, and when she asked the cause, then Else told her how the future possible child might be killed as soon as it was big enough to be sent to draw beer, by the pickaxe falling on it. Then the mother at once exclaimed, "Our Else is clever indeed!" and, sitting down, she wept with the rest.

Upstairs the husband waited a little while, but as his wife did not return, and as his thirst constantly increased, he said, "I must go down to the cellar myself, and see what has become of Else." And when he came into the cellar, and found them all sitting and weeping together, he was told that it was all owing to the child that Else might possibly have, and the possibility of its being killed by the pickaxe so happening to fall just at the time the child might be sitting underneath it drawing beer; and when he heard all this, he cried, "How clever is our Else!" and sitting down, he joined his tears to theirs.

The intended bridegroom stayed upstairs by himself a long time, but as nobody came back to him, he thought he would go himself and see what they were all about. And there he found all five lamenting and crying most pitifully, each one louder than the other.

"What misfortune has happened?" cried he.

"O my dear Hans," said Else, "if we marry and have a child, and it grows big, and we send it down here to draw beer, perhaps that pickaxe which has been left sticking up there might fall down on the child's head and kill it; and how can we help crying at that!"

"Now," said Hans, "I cannot think that greater sense than that could be wanted in my household; so as you are so clever, Else, I will have you for my wife," and taking her by the hand he led her upstairs, and they had the wedding at once.

Element Focus: Plot

What is the likelihood that Else will really be a sensible wife for Hans, given the events in this story? Support your answer.

Excerpt from

The Story of Doctor Dolittle

by Hugh Lofting

The parrot taught him. And the doctor learned the language of the animals. He could talk to them. And he could understand everything they said. Then he stopped being a people's doctor.

Old ladies began to bring him their pet dogs who had eaten too much cake. And farmers came many miles to show him sick cows and sheep.

One day a plow horse was brought to him. The poor thing was very glad to find a man who could talk in horse language.

"You know, Doctor," said the horse, "that vet over the hill knows nothing. He has been treating me six weeks now. He thinks I have spavins. What I need is GLASSES. I am going blind in one eye. There is no reason why horses should not wear glasses. It is just the same as people. But that stupid man never looked at my eyes. He kept giving me big pills. I tried to tell him. But he couldn't understand a word I said. What I need is glasses."

"Of course. Of course," said the doctor. "I will get you some."

"I want a pair like yours," said the horse. "But make them green. They will keep the sun out of my eyes. That will help while I plow the Fifty-Acre Field."

"Yes," said the doctor. "You shall have green ones."

"You know, the trouble is, Sir," said the horse. The doctor opened the front door to let him out. "The trouble is that ANYBODY thinks he can doctor animals. This is just because we don't complain. As a matter of fact, it takes a much smarter man to be a really good animal doctor. It is harder than being a good people's doctor. My farmer's boy thinks he knows all about horses. I wish you could see him. His face is so fat! He looks like he has no eyes. He has got less brain than a bug. He tried to put a mustard plaster on me last week."

"Where did he put it?" asked the doctor.

"Oh, he didn't put it anywhere. Not on me," said the horse. "He tried to. So I kicked him into the duck pond."

"Well, well!" said the doctor.

"I am pretty quiet," said the horse. "I am very patient with people. I do not make much fuss. But things were bad enough. That vet was giving me the wrong medicine. Then that red-faced booby started to mess with me! I just couldn't bear it anymore."

"Did you hurt the boy much?" asked the doctor.

"Oh, no," said the horse. "I kicked him in the right place. The vet is looking after him now. When will my glasses be ready?"

"I'll have them for you next week," said the doctor. "Come in on Tuesday. Good morning!"

Then John Dolittle got a fine, big pair of green glasses. And the plow horse stopped going blind in one eye. He could see as well as ever.

Soon it was common to see farm animals wearing glasses. A blind horse was a thing unknown.

And so it was with all the other animals that were brought to him. They soon found that he could talk their language. Then they told him where the pain was. They said how they felt. Then it was easy for him to cure them.

Element Focus: Plot

In what ways does Dr. Dolittle help
the animals in the passage?

Excerpt from

The Story of Doctor Dolittle

by Hugh Lofting

After a while, with the parrot's help, the doctor got to learn the language of the animals. He learned so well that he could talk to them himself. And he could understand everything they said. Then he gave up being a people's doctor altogether.

Old ladies began to bring him their pet pugs and poodles who had eaten too much cake. And farmers came many miles to show him sick cows and sheep.

One day a plow horse was brought to him. The poor thing was very delighted to find a man who could talk in horse language.

"You know, Doctor," said the horse, "that vet over the hill knows nothing. He has been treating me six weeks now—for spavins. What I need is GLASSES. I am going blind in one eye. There's no reason why horses shouldn't wear glasses. It is just the same as people. But that senseless man never even looked at my eyes. He kept on giving me big pills. I tried to tell him. But he couldn't understand a word I said. What I need is glasses."

"Of course—of course," said the doctor. "I'll get you some at once."

"I would like a pair like yours," said the horse—"only green. They'll keep the sun out of my eyes. That will help while I'm plowing the Fifty-Acre Field."

"Of course," said the doctor. "Green ones you shall have."

"You know, the misfortune is, Sir," said the plow horse. The doctor opened the front door to let him out. "The trouble is that ANYBODY thinks he can doctor animals. This is just because the animals don't complain. As a matter of fact, it takes a much cleverer man to be a really worthy animal doctor than it does to be a good people's doctor. My farmer's boy thinks he knows all about horses. I wish you could see him. His face is so fat he looks as though he has no eyes. He has got as much brain as a potato bug. He tried to put a mustard plaster on me last week."

"Where did he put it?" enquired the doctor.

"Oh, he didn't put it anywhere—on me," said the horse. "He only tried to. I kicked him into the duck pond."

"Well, well!" said the doctor.

"I'm a pretty quiet creature as a rule," said the horse—"I am very patient with people. I don't make much fuss. But it was bad enough with that vet giving me the wrong medicine. When that red-faced booby started to mess with me, I just couldn't bear it anymore."

"Did you hurt the boy much?" asked the doctor.

"Oh, no," said the horse. "I kicked him in the accurate place. The vet is observing after him now. When will my glasses be complete?"

"I'll have them for you next week," said the doctor. "Come in again Tuesday. Good morning!"

Then John Dolittle got a fine, big pair of green glasses. And the plow horse stopped going blind in one eye. He could see as well as ever.

Soon it was common to see farm animals wearing glasses near Puddleby. A blind horse was a thing unknown.

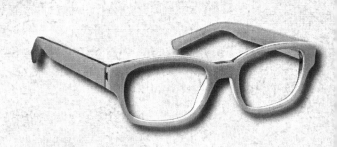

And so it was with all the other animals that were brought to him. As soon as they found that he could talk their language, they told him where the pain was and how they felt. Of course, it was easy for him to cure them.

Element Focus: Plot

Describe the ways that Dr. Dolittle is able to help the animals in the passage.

The Story of Doctor Dolittle

by Hugh Lofting

After some time, with the parrot's assistance, the doctor came to learn the language of the animals so fluently that he could speak to them himself and understand everything they said. At that point, he retired from being a people's doctor altogether and focused entirely on his animal practice.

Old ladies began to bring him their pet pugs and poodles who had consumed too much cake; and farmers journeyed many miles to bring him their ailing cows and sheep.

One day a plow horse was brought to him; and the poor thing was terribly pleased to discover a human who could communicate fluently in horse language.

"You know, Doctor," complained the horse, "that vet over the hill knows nothing at all. He has been treating me six weeks now—for spavins—when what I need is SPECTACLES. I am going blind in one eye. There's no reason why horses shouldn't wear glasses, the same as people, but that imbecile over the hill never even bothered to examine my eyes. He insisted on giving me big pills. I tried to tell him; but he couldn't understand a word of horse language. What I need is spectacles."

"Of course—of course," replied the doctor reassuringly. "I'll get you some at once."

"I would like a pair similar to yours," said the horse—"only green. They'll protect my eyes from the sun while I'm plowing the Fifty-Acre Field."

"Certainly," agreed the doctor immediately. "Green ones you shall have."

"You know, the trouble is, Sir," confided the plow horse as the doctor opened the front door to let him out—"the trouble is that ANYBODY thinks he can doctor animals—just because the animals don't complain. As a matter of fact, it takes a much cleverer man to be a really good animal doctor than it does to be a good people's doctor. My farmer's boy thinks he knows all about horses. I wish you could see him—his face is so fat he looks as though he has no eyes—and he has got only as much brain as a potato bug. He tried to put a mustard plaster on me last week."

"Where did he put it?" inquired the doctor.

"Oh, he didn't put it anywhere—on me," relayed the horse. "He tried to, but I kicked him into the duck pond."

"Well, well!" exclaimed the doctor, not entirely disapprovingly.

"I'm a pretty quiet creature as a rule," said the horse—"generally very patient with people—don't make much fuss. But it was bad enough to have that vet giving me the wrong medicine, and when that red-faced booby started to monkey with me, I just couldn't bear it anymore."

"Did you hurt the boy much?" asked the doctor with polite concern.

"Oh, no," assured the horse. "I kicked him in the right place. The vet's looking after him now. When will my glasses be ready?"

"I'll have them ready for you next week," said the doctor. "Come in again Tuesday—good morning!"

Then John Dolittle got a fine, big pair of green spectacles; and the plow-horse stopped going blind in one eye and could see as well as ever.

And soon it became commonplace to observe farm animals wearing glasses in the country round Puddleby; and, indeed, a blind horse was a thing unknown.

And so it was with all the other animals that were brought to him. As soon as they found that he could speak their language, they told him where the pain was and how they felt, and, of course, it was easy for him to cure them.

Element Focus: Plot

Explain several reasons why the animals are not satisfied with normal animal doctors.
What problems does this create?

The Story of Doctor Dolittle

by Hugh Lofting

After some time—with the parrot's assistance—the doctor came to discover the language of the animals so fluently that he could speak to them himself and understand everything they said. At that point, he retired from being a people's doctor altogether and concentrated entirely on his animal practice.

Old ladies began to bring him their pet pugs and poodles who had consumed too much cake; and farmers journeyed many miles to bring him their ailing cows and sheep.

One day a plow horse was brought to him; and the poor creature was terribly pleased to discover a human who could communicate effortlessly in horse language.

"You know, Doctor," complained the horse, "that vet over the hill knows nothing at all. He has been doctoring me for six weeks now—for spavins—when what I need is SPECTACLES. I'm going blind in one eye. There's no reason why horses shouldn't wear glasses, the same as people—that imbecile over the hill never even bothered to examine my eyes. He insisted on giving me big pills. I tried to tell him; but he couldn't comprehend a word of horse language. What I need is spectacles."

"Of course—of course," responded the doctor reassuringly. "I'll get you some at once."

"I would like a pair similar to yours," said the horse—"only green. They'll guard my eyes from the sun while I'm plowing the Fifty-Acre Field."

"Certainly," agreed the doctor instantaneously. "Green ones you shall have."

"You know, the trouble is, Sir," confided the plow horse as the doctor unfastened the front door to let him out—"the trouble is that ANYBODY thinks he can doctor animals—just because the animals don't criticize. As a matter of fact, it takes a much cleverer man to be a really reputable animal doctor than it does to be a good people's doctor. My farmer's boy thinks he knows all about horses. I wish you could see him—his face is so pudgy he looks as though he has no eyes—and he has got only as much brain as a potato bug. He tried to put a mustard plaster on me last week."

"Where did he put it?" inquired the doctor.

"Oh, he didn't put it anywhere—on me," relayed the horse. "He tried to, but I kicked him into the duck pond."

"Well, well!" exclaimed the doctor, not entirely disapprovingly.

"I'm a pretty peaceful creature as a rule," said the horse—"generally very patient with people—don't make much fuss. But it was bad enough to have that vet giving me the wrong medicine, and when that red-faced booby started to monkey with me, I just couldn't bear it anymore."

"Did you hurt the boy much?" asked the doctor with polite concern.

"Oh, no," assured the horse. "I kicked him in the right place. The vet's looking after him now. When will my glasses be ready?"

"I'll have them ready for you next week," said the doctor. "Come in again Tuesday—good morning!"

Then John Dolittle got a fine, big pair of green spectacles; and the plow-horse stopped going blind in one eye and could see as well as ever.

And soon it became commonplace to observe farm animals wearing glasses in the country round Puddleby; and, indeed, a blind horse was a thing unknown.

And so it was with all the other animals that were brought to him. As soon as they found that he could speak their language, they told him where the pain was and how they felt, and, of course, it was easy for him to cure them.

Element Focus: Plot

What problems are created when humans who do not speak animal languages try to help sick animals?

#50988—Leveled Texts for Classic Fiction: Humor

Excerpt from

Tales from Shakespeare

by Charles and Mary Lamb

[As a trick, Oberon has put juice from a magical flower in Titania's eyes. This casts a spell. It makes it so she will fall madly in love with the first person she sees....]

Oberon was the king of the fairies. Titania was the queen. In the woods they held midnight parties with their group of tiny followers. But this little king and queen were having a disagreement. They never met by moonlight. They never met in shady paths of the pleasant wood. But they would always argue. All their fairy elves would hide in acorn cups from fear. They argued because Titania would not give Oberon a little changeling boy. The child's mother had been Titania's friend. When she died, the fairy queen stole the baby from its nurse. The fairy brought him up in the woods.

Titania was still sleeping. Oberon saw a clown close by. This clown had lost his way in the wood. He was asleep, too. "This fellow," said the king, "will be my Titania's true love." The king put a donkey's head over the clown's. It seemed to fit him as well as if it had grown there. Oberon did this very gently. But the clown woke up. He stood up. But he did not know what Oberon had done. So, he went toward the bed of leaves where the queen slept.

"Ah, what angel is that I see?" said Titania. She was just opening her eyes. The juice of the little flower had started to work. "Are you as wise as you are beautiful?"

"Why, mistress," said the foolish clown, "all I need is enough brains to get out of the woods. That would be fine with me."

"Do not say you want to leave the woods," said the love-struck queen. "I am no common spirit. I love you. Go with me! I will give you fairies to wait on you." She then called four of her fairies. One was named Peas-blossom. Another was called Cobweb. The third was Moth. And the last was Mustard-seed.

"Serve this sweet gentleman," said the queen, "Hop in his walks! Skip in his sight! Feed him grapes! Feed him apricots! Steal the honey bags from the bees for him. Come, sit with me," said she to the clown. "Let me play with your lovely hairy cheeks! You are such a beautiful donkey! Let me kiss your handsome large ears! You are my gentle joy."

"Where is Peas-blossom?" said the donkey-headed clown. He did not care much for the queen's love. But he was very proud of his new servants.

"Here, sir," said little Peas-blossom.

"Scratch my head," said the clown. "Where is Cobweb?"

"Here, sir," said Cobweb.

"Good Mr. Cobweb," said the foolish clown. "Kill me the red humblebee on the top of that flower! And bring me the honey bag. Do not risk yourself too much. And be careful not to break the honey bag. I should be sorry to have you overflown with a honey bag. Where is Mustard-seed?"

"Here, sir," said Mustard-seed. "What is your will?"

"Nothing," said the clown. "Only do help Mr. Peas-blossom to scratch. I must go to a barbers! I think I am very hairy about the face."

"My sweet love," said the queen, "what will you have to eat? I have a brave fairy who can steal the squirrel's hoard. He can fetch you some new nuts."

"I would like a handful of dried peas," said the clown. With his donkey's head he wanted donkey's food. "But please, keep your people from bothering me. I want to sleep."

"Sleep then," said the queen. "I will cuddle you in my arms. Oh, how I love you! How I dote upon you!"

Element Focus: Plot

What other outcomes could have been possible and why?

Excerpt from

Tales from Shakespeare

by Charles and Mary Lamb

[As a trick, Oberon has put juice from a magical flower in Titania's eyes. This casts a spell so she will fall madly in love with the first person she might see....]

Oberon was the king of the fairies. Titania was the queen. In this wood, they held midnight parties with their tiny group of followers. Between this little king and queen of sprites there was, at this time, a sad disagreement. They never met by moonlight in the shady walk of this pleasant wood. But, they would always argue. All their fairy elves would creep into acorn cups and hide themselves for fear. The cause of this unhappy disagreement was Titania's refusing to give Oberon a little changeling boy. The child's mother had been Titania's friend. Upon her death, the fairy queen stole the child from its nurse. The fairy brought him up in the woods.

Titania was still sleeping. Oberon saw a clown near her. This clown had lost his way in the wood. He was asleep, too. "This fellow," said the king, "will be my Titania's true love." The king placed a donkey's head over the clown's. It seemed to fit him as well as if it had grown there. Oberon did this very gently. But still, it awakened the clown. He rose up. But he did not know what Oberon had done to him. So he went toward the bower where the fairy queen slept.

"Ah, what angel is that I see?" said Titania. She was just opening her eyes. The juice of the little purple flower had begun to take effect. "Are you as wise as you are beautiful?"

"Why, mistress," said the foolish clown, "if I have enough wit to find the way out of this wood, I have all I need."

"Do not desire to leave the woods," said the love-struck queen. "I am no common spirit. I love you. Go with me! I will give you fairies to wait on you." She then called four of her fairies. One was named Peas-blossom. Another was called Cobweb. The third was Moth. And the last was Mustard-seed.

"Attend," said the queen, "upon this sweet gentleman. Hop in his walks! Skip in his sight! Feed him with grapes and apricots. Steal for him the honey bags from the bees. Come, sit with me," said she to the clown. "Let me play with your lovely hairy cheeks! You are such a beautiful donkey! Let me kiss your handsome large ears! You are my gentle joy."

"Where is Peas-blossom?" said the donkey-headed clown. He did not have much use for the fairy queen's courtship. But he was very proud of his new servants.

"Here, sir," said little Peas-blossom.

"Scratch my head," said the clown. "Where is Cobweb?"

"Here, sir," said Cobweb.

"Good Mr. Cobweb," said the foolish clown. "Kill me the red humblebee on the top of that thistle there! And, good Mr. Cobweb, bring me the honey bag. Do not fret yourself too much in the action, Mr. Cobweb. And take care the honey bag break not. I should be sorry to have you overflown with a honey bag. Where is Mustard-seed?"

"Here, sir," said Mustard-seed. "What is your will?"

"Nothing," said the clown, "good Mr. Mustard-seed, but to help Mr. Peas-blossom to scratch. I must go to a barbers, Mr. Mustard-seed! I think I am very hairy about the face."

"My sweet love," said the queen, "what will you have to eat? I have a brave fairy who shall seek the squirrel's hoard. He can fetch you some new nuts."

"I would like a handful of dried peas," said the clown. With his donkey's head he had got a donkey's appetite. "But I pray, let none of your people disturb me. I have a mind to sleep."

"Sleep then," said the queen. "I will cuddle you in my arms. Oh, how I love you! How I dote upon you!"

Element Focus: Plot

Describe how Titania's refusal to give Oberon the changeling boy leads to a clown with a donkey's head being served by a group of fairies.

Excerpt from

Tales from Shakespeare

by Charles and Mary Lamb

[As a trick, Oberon has put juice from a magical flower in Titania's eyes so that she will fall madly in love with the first person she might gaze upon....]

Oberon the king, and Titania the queen of the fairies, with all their tiny train of followers, in this wood held their midnight revels. Between this little king and queen of sprites there happened, at this time, a sad disagreement; they never met by moonlight in the shady walk of this pleasant wood but they were quarreling, till all their fairy elves would creep into acorn cups and hide themselves for fear. The cause of this unhappy disagreement was Titania's refusing to give Oberon a little changeling boy, whose mother had been Titania's friend; and upon her death the fairy queen stole the child from its nurse and brought him up in the woods.

Titania was still sleeping, and Oberon, saw a clown near her who had lost his way in the wood and was likewise asleep. "This fellow," said he, "shall be my Titania's true love;" and clapping a donkey's head over the clown's, it seemed to fit him as well as if it had grown upon his own shoulders. Though Oberon fixed a donkey's head on very gently, it awakened him, and, rising up, unconscious of what Oberon had done to him, he went toward the bower where the fairy queen slept.

"Ah, what angel is that I see?" said Titania, opening her eyes, and the juice of the little purple flower beginning to take effect. "Are you as wise as you are beautiful?"

"Why, mistress," said the foolish clown, "if I have wit enough to find the way out of this wood, I have enough to serve my turn."

"Out of the wood do not desire to go," said the enamoured queen. "I am a spirit of no common rate. I love you. Go with me, and I will give you fairies to attend upon you." She then called four of her fairies. Their names were Peas-blossom, Cobweb, Moth, and Mustard-seed.

"Attend," said the queen, "upon this sweet gentleman. Hop in his walks and gambol in his sight; feed him with grapes and apricots, and steal for him the honey bags from the bees. Come, sit with me," said she to the clown, "and let me play with your amiable hairy cheeks, my beautiful donkey! And kiss your fair large ears, my gentle joy."

"Where is Peas-blossom?" said the donkey-headed clown, not much regarding the fairy queen's courtship, but very proud of his new attendants.

"Here, sir," said little Peas-blossom.

"Scratch my head," said the clown. "Where is Cobweb?"

"Here, sir," said Cobweb.

"Good Mr. Cobweb," said the foolish clown, "kill me the red humblebee on the top of that thistle yonder; and, good Mr. Cobweb, bring me the honey bag. Do not fret yourself too much in the action, Mr. Cobweb, and take care the honey bag break not; I should be sorry to have you overflown with a honey bag. Where is Mustard-seed?"

"Here, sir," said Mustard-seed. "What is your will?"

"Nothing," said the clown, "good Mr. Mustard-seed, but to help Mr. Peas-blossom to scratch; I must go to a barber's, Mr. Mustard-seed, for methinks I am marvelous hairy about the face."

"My sweet love," said the queen, "what will you have to eat? I have a venturous fairy shall seek the squirrel's hoard, and fetch you some new nuts."

"I had rather have a handful of dried peas," said the clown, who with his donkey's head had got a donkey's appetite. "But, I pray, let none of your people disturb me, for I have a mind to sleep."

"Sleep, then," said the queen, "and I will wind you in my arms. Oh, how I love you! How I dote upon you!"

Element Focus: Plot

Describe several consequences that result from Oberon's jealousy about Titania's changeling boy.

Tales from Shakespeare

by Charles and Mary Lamb

[As a trick, Oberon has put juice from a magical flower in Titania's eyes so that she will fall madly in love with the first person she might gaze upon....]

Oberon the king, and Titania the queen of the fairies, with all their tiny train of followers, in this wood held their midnight revels. Between this little king and queen of sprites there happened, at this time, a sad disagreement; they never met by moonlight in the shady walk of this pleasant wood but they were quarreling, till all their fairy elves would creep into acorn cups and hide themselves for fear. The cause of this unhappy disagreement was Titania's refusing to give Oberon a little changeling boy, whose mother had been Titania's friend. Upon her passing, the fairy queen stole the child from its nurse and proceeded to bring him to the woods.

Titania was still sleeping, and Oberon, saw a clown near her who had lost his way in the wood and was likewise asleep. "This fellow," said he, "shall be my Titania's true love;" and clapping a donkey's head over the clown's, it seemed to fit him as well as if it had grown upon his own shoulders. Though Oberon fixed a donkey's head on very gently; it awakened him, and rising up, unconscious of what Oberon had done to him, he went toward the bower where the fairy queen slept.

"Ah, what angel is that I see?" said Titania, opening her eyes, and the juice of the little purple flower beginning to take effect. "Are you as wise as you are beautiful?"

"Why, mistress," said the foolish clown, "if I have intelligence enough to find a method out of this wood, I have enough to operate my turn."

"Out of the wood do not desire to go," said the enamoured queen. "I am a spirit of no common rate. I love you—proceed with me and I will give you fairies to attend upon you." She then shouted four of her fairies—their names were Peas-blossom, Cobweb, Moth, and Mustard-seed.

"Attend," said the queen, "upon this sweet gentleman. Hop in his walks and gambol in his sight; feed him with grapes and apricots, and steal for him the honey bags from the bees. Come, sit with me," said she to the clown, "and let me play with your amiable hairy cheeks, my beautiful donkey! And kiss your fair large ears, my temperate joy."

"Where is Peas-blossom?" said the donkey-headed clown, not much regarding the fairy queen's courtship, but very satisfied of his new attendants.

"Here, sir," said little Peas-blossom.

"Scratch my head," said the clown. "Where is Cobweb?"

"Present, sir," said Cobweb.

"Good Mr. Cobweb," said the foolish clown, "kill me the red humblebee on the top of that thistle yonder; and, good Mr. Cobweb, bring me the honey bag. Do not agonize yourself too much in the action, Mr. Cobweb, and take care the honey bag break not; I should be sorry to have you overflown with a honey bag. Where is Mustard-seed?"

"Present, sir," said Mustard-seed. "What's your will?"

"Nothing," said the clown, "good Mr. Mustard-seed, but to help Mr. Peas-blossom to scratch; I must go to a barber's, Mr. Mustard-seed, for methinks I am marvelous hairy about the face."

"My sweet love," said the queen, "what will you have to eat? I have a venturous fairy shall seek the squirrel's hoard, and fetch you some new nuts."

"I had rather have a handful of dried peas," said the clown, who with his donkey's head had got a donkey's appetite. "But, I pray, let none of your people disturb me, for I have a mind to sleep."

"Sleep, then," said the queen, "and I will wind you in my arms. Oh, how I love you! How I dote upon you!"

Element Focus: Plot

Explain how the string of events started by Oberon's jealousy of Titania's changeling boy provides humor in the story.

Excerpt from

The Celebrated Jumping Frog of Calaveras County

by Mark Twain

You never see a frog so modest as he was. Though he was so gifted. And when it come to fair and square jumping on a dead level? He could get over more ground at one straddle than any animal of his breed you ever see. Jumping on a dead level was his strong suit, you understand. And when it come to that, Smiley would bet any money on him. Smiley was monstrous proud of his frog. And well he might be! Fellers that had traveled and been everywheres all said he laid over any frog that ever *they* see.

Well, Smiley kept the beast in a little woven box. And he used to fetch him downtown sometimes. Then he would look for a bet. One day a feller—a stranger in the camp, he was—come across him with his box. He says:

"What might be that you've got in the box?"

And Smiley says, sorter indifferent-like, "It might be a parrot. Or it might be a canary, maybe. But it ain't. It's only just a frog."

And the feller took it. And he looked at it careful. And he turned it round this way and that. And he says, "Hmm—so it is. Well, what's *he* good for?"

"Well," Smiley says, easy and careless, "he's good enough for *one* thing. He can outjump any frog in Calaveras County."

The feller took the box again. He took another long, careful look. Then he give it back to Smiley. "Well," he says, "I don't see no points about that frog that's any better than any other frog."

"Maybe you don't," Smiley says. "Maybe you understand frogs. And maybe you don't understand 'em. Maybe you've had experience. And maybe you are only an amateur. Anyways, I have *my* opinion. And I'll risk forty dollars on it. I say he can out-jump any frog in Calaveras County."

And the feller studied a minute. Then he says, kinder sad like, "Well, I'm only a stranger here. I ain't got no frog. But if I had a frog, I'd bet you."

And then Smiley says, "That is all right. That is all right. You hold my box a minute. I'll go and get you a frog." And so the feller took the box. He put up his forty dollars along with Smiley's. Then he set down to wait.

So he set there a good while thinking to his-self. And then he got the frog out. He pried his mouth open. He took a teaspoon and filled him full of quail shot. He *filled* him pretty near up to his chin! And he set him on the floor. Smiley he went to the swamp. He slopped around in the mud for a long time. And finally he ketched a frog. He fetched it in, and give it to this feller. He says:

"Now, if you're ready, set him alongside of Daniel. Put his forepaws just even with Daniel's. I'll give the word." Then he says, "One—two—three—*git!*" Him and the feller touched up the frogs from behind. The new frog hopped off lively. But Daniel give a heave. He hoisted up his shoulders—so—like a Frenchman. But it wasn't no use. He couldn't budge. He was planted as solid as a church. He couldn't no more stir than if he was anchored out. Smiley was a good deal surprised. And he was disgusted, too! But, he didn't have no idea what the matter was, of course.

The feller took the money and started away. And when he was going out at the door, he sorter jerked his thumb over his shoulder—so—at Daniel. He says again, "Well," he says, "*I don't see no points about that frog that's any better than any other frog.*"

Smiley, he stood scratching his head. He looks down at Daniel a long time. And at last says, "I do wonder what that frog throwed off for. I wonder if there ain't something the matter with him. He appears to look mighty baggy, somehow." And he ketched Daniel up by the nape of the neck. As he hefted him, he says, "Why, blame my cats if he don't weigh five pounds!" And he turned him upside down. He belched out a double handful of shot. And then he see how it was! And he was the maddest man. He set the frog down! He took out after that feller! But, he never ketched him.

Element Focus: Language Usage

Describe the choice of words Mark Twain used in this story. Explain several reasons he might have chosen to use words in this unusual way.

Excerpt from

The Celebrated Jumping Frog of Calaveras County

by Mark Twain

You never see a frog so modest and straightfor'ard as he was. Though he was so gifted. And what when it come to fair and square jumping on a dead level? He could get over more ground at one straddle than any animal of his breed you ever see. Jumping on a dead level was his strong suit, you understand. And when it come to that, Smiley would ante up money on him as long as he had a red. Smiley was monstrous proud of his frog. And well he might be! For fellers that had traveled and been everywheres, all said he laid over any frog that ever *they* see.

Well, Smiley kep' the beast in a little lattice box. And he used to fetch him downtown sometimes and lay for a bet. One day a feller—a stranger in the camp, he was—come acrost him with his box. He says:

"What might be that you've got in the box?"

And Smiley says, sorter indifferent-like, "It might be a parrot. Or it might be a canary, maybe. But it ain't—it's only just a frog."

And the feller took it. And he looked at it careful. And he turned it round this way and that. And he says, "H'm—so 'tis. Well, what's *he* good for?"

"Well," Smiley says, easy and careless, "he's good enough for *one* thing, I should judge. He can outjump any frog in Calaveras County."

The feller took the box again, and took another long, particular look, and give it back to Smiley, and says, very deliberate, "Well," he says, "I don't see no p'ints about that frog that's any better'n any other frog."

"Maybe you don't," Smiley says. "Maybe you understand frogs and maybe you don't understand 'em. Maybe you've had experience. And maybe you ain't only a amateur, as it were. Anyways, I've got *my* opinion. And I'll risk forty dollars that he can outjump any frog in Calaveras County."

And the feller studied a minute. Then he says, kinder sad like, "Well, I'm only a stranger here, and I ain't got no frog. But if I had a frog, I'd bet you."

And then Smiley says, "That's all right—that's all right—if you'll hold my box a minute, I'll go and get you a frog." And so the feller took the box. He put up his forty dollars along with Smiley's, and set down to wait.

So he set there a good while thinking and thinking to his-self. And then he got the frog out and prized his mouth open. He took a teaspoon and filled him full of quail shot—filled him pretty near up to his chin—and set him on the floor. Smiley, he went to the swamp and slopped around in the mud for a long time. And finally he ketched a frog, and fetched him in, and give him to this feller, and says:

"Now, if you're ready, set him alongside of Dan'l, with his forepaws just even with Dan'l's. I'll give the word." Then he says, "One—two—three—*git!*" and him and the feller touched up the frogs from behind. The new frog hopped off lively. But Dan'l give a heave, and hysted up his shoulders—so—like a Frenchman, but it warn't no use—he couldn't budge. He was planted as solid as a church. He couldn't no more stir than if he was anchored out. Smiley was a good deal surprised, and he was disgusted, too! But, he didn't have no idea what the matter was, of course.

The feller took the money and started away. And when he was going out at the door, he sorter jerked his thumb over his shoulder—so—at Dan'l. He says again, very deliberate, "Well," he says, "*I don't see no p'ints about that frog that's any better'n any other frog.*"

Smiley, he stood scratching his head and looking down at Dan'l a long time. And at last says, "I do wonder what in the nation that frog throwed off for. I wonder if there ain't something the matter with him. He 'pears to look mighty baggy, somehow." And he ketched Dan'l up by the nape of the neck. As he hefted him, he says, "Why, blame my cats if he don't weigh five pounds!" And he turned him upside down. He belched out a double handful of shot. And then he see how it was! And he was the maddest man. He set the frog down and took out after that feller! But, he never ketched him.

Element Focus: Language Usage

Mark Twain wrote this story using slang that his characters might use. How might you write this story differently if it were supposed to take place now?

Excerpt from

The Celebrated Jumping Frog of Calaveras County

by Mark Twain

You never see a frog so modest and straightfor'ard as he was. Though he was so gifted. And when it come to fair and square jumping on a dead level, he could get over more ground at one straddle than any animal of his breed you ever see. Jumping on a dead level was his strong suit, you understand. And when it come to that, Smiley would ante up money on him as long as he had a red. Smiley was monstrous proud of his frog. And well he might be! For fellers that had traveled and been everywheres, all said he laid over any frog that ever *they* see.

Well, Smiley kep' the beast in a little lattice box. And he used to fetch him downtown sometimes and lay for a bet. One day a feller—a stranger in the camp, he was—come acrost him with his box. He says:

"What might be that you've got in the box?"

And Smiley says, sorter indifferent-like, "It might be a parrot, or it might be a canary, maybe. But it ain't—it's only just a frog."

And the feller took it. And he looked at it careful. And he turned it round this way and that. And he says, "H'm—so 'tis. Well, what's *he* good for?"

"Well," Smiley says, easy and careless, "he's good enough for *one* thing, I should judge—he can outjump any frog in Calaveras County."

The feller took the box again, and took another long, particular look, and give it back to Smiley, and says, very deliberate, "Well," he says, "I don't see no p'ints about that frog that's any better'n any other frog."

"Maybe you don't," Smiley says. "Maybe you understand frogs and maybe you don't understand 'em. Maybe you've had experience. And maybe you ain't only a amateur, as it were. Anyways, I've got *my* opinion. And I'll risk forty dollars that he can outjump any frog in Calaveras County."

And the feller studied a minute. Then he says, kinder sad like, "Well, I'm only a stranger here, and I ain't got no frog. But if I had a frog, I'd bet you."

And then Smiley says, "That's all right—that's all right—if you'll hold my box a minute, I'll go and get you a frog." And so the feller took the box. He put up his forty dollars along with Smiley's, and set down to wait.

So he set there a good while thinking and thinking to his-self. And then he got the frog out and prized his mouth open and took a teaspoon and filled him full of quail shot—filled him pretty near up to his chin—and set him on the floor. Smiley, he went to the swamp and slopped around in the mud for a long time. And finally he ketched a frog, and fetched him in, and give him to this feller, and says:

"Now, if you're ready, set him alongside of Dan'l, with his forepaws just even with Dan'l's, and I'll give the word." Then he says, "One—two—three—*git!*" and him and the feller touched up the frogs from behind, and the new frog hopped off lively, but Dan'l give a heave, and hysted up his shoulders—so—like a Frenchman, but it warn't no use—he couldn't budge; he was planted as solid as a church, and he couldn't no more stir than if he was anchored out. Smiley was a good deal surprised, and he was disgusted, too, but he didn't have no idea what the matter was, of course.

The feller took the money and started away; and when he was going out at the door, he sorter jerked his thumb over his shoulder—so—at Dan'l, and says again, very deliberate, "Well," he says, "*I* don't see no p'ints about that frog that's any better'n any other frog."

Smiley, he stood scratching his head and looking down at Dan'l a long time. And at last says, "I do wonder what in the nation that frog throwed off for. I wonder if there ain't something the matter with him. He 'pears to look mighty baggy, somehow." And he ketched Dan'l up by the nape of the neck, and hefted him, and says, "Why, blame my cats if he don't weigh five pounds!" and turned him upside down and he belched out a double handful of shot. And then he see how it was, and he was the maddest man—he set the frog down and took out after that feller, but he never ketched him.

Element Focus: Language Usage

What if Mark Twain had written this story without trying to copy the slang of the characters? How would that affect the humor of the tale?

Excerpt from

The Celebrated Jumping Frog of Calaveras County

by Mark Twain

You never see a frog so modest and straightfor'ard as he was, for all he was so gifted. And when it come to fair and square jumping on a dead level, he could get over more ground at one straddle than any animal of his breed you ever see. Jumping on a dead level was his strong suit, you understand. And when it come to that, Smiley would ante up money on him as long as he had a red. Smiley was monstrous proud of his frog. And well he might be, for fellers that had traveled and been everywheres, all said he laid over any frog that ever *they* see.

Well, Smiley kep' the beast in a little lattice box, and he used to fetch him downtown sometimes and lay for a bet. One day a feller—a stranger in the camp, he was—come acrost him with his box, and says:

"What might be that you've got in the box?"

And Smiley says, sorter indifferent-like, "It might be a parrot, or it might be a canary, maybe, but it ain't—it's only just a frog."

And the feller took it, and looked at it careful, and turned it round this way and that, and says, "H'm—so 'tis. Well, what's *he* good for?"

"Well," Smiley says, easy and careless, "he's good enough for *one* thing, I should judge—he can outjump any frog in Calaveras county."

The feller took the box again, and took another long, particular look, and give it back to Smiley, and says, very deliberate, "Well," he says, "I don't see no p'ints about that frog that's any better'n any other frog."

"Maybe you don't," Smiley says. "Maybe you understand frogs and maybe you don't understand 'em. Maybe you've had experience, and maybe you ain't only a amature, as it were. Anyways, I've got *my* opinion and I'll risk forty dollars that he can outjump any frog in Calaveras County."

And the feller studied a minute, and then says, kinder sad like, "Well, I'm only a stranger here, and I ain't got no frog; but if I had a frog, I'd bet you."

And then Smiley says, "That's all right—that's all right—if you'll hold my box a minute, I'll go and get you a frog." And so the feller took the box, and put up his forty dollars along with Smiley's, and set down to wait.

So he set there a good while thinking and thinking to his-self, and then he got the frog out and prized his mouth open and took a teaspoon and filled him full of quail shot—filled! Him pretty near up to his chin—and set him on the floor. Smiley he went to the swamp and slopped around in the mud for a long time, and finally he ketched a frog, and fetched him in, and give him to this feller, and says:

"Now, if you're ready, set him alongside of Dan'l, with his forepaws just even with Dan'l's, and I'll give the word." Then he says, "One—two—three—*git*!" and him and the feller touched up the frogs from behind, and the new frog hopped off lively, but Dan'l give a heave, and hysted up his shoulders—so—like a Frenchman, but it warn't no use—he couldn't budge; he was planted as solid as a church, and he couldn't no more stir than if he was anchored out. Smiley was a good deal surprised, and he was disgusted too, but he didn't have no idea what the matter was, of course.

The feller took the money and started away; and when he was going out at the door, he sorter jerked his thumb over his shoulder—so—at Dan'l, and says again, very deliberate, "Well," he says, "*I don't see no p'ints about that frog that's any better'n any other frog.*"

Smiley he stood scratching his head and looking down at Dan'l a long time. And at last says, "I do wonder what in the nation that frog throwed off for. I wonder if there ain't something the matter with him. He 'pears to look mighty baggy, somehow." And he ketched Dan'l up by the nap of the neck, and hefted him, and says, "Why blame my cats if he don't weigh five pounds!" and turned him upside down and he belched out a double handful of shot. And then he see how it was, and he was the maddest man—he set the frog down and took out after that feller, but he never ketched him.

Element Focus: Language Usage

In what ways did Mark Twain's choice to use language mimicking the slang of his characters contribute to the humorous tone of the story?

Excerpt from

How the Camel Got His Hump

by Rudyard Kippling

In the beginning of years, when the world was so new and all, the animals were just starting to work for Man. There was a Camel. He lived in the middle of a Howling Desert. This was because he did not want to work. And he was a howler himself. So he ate sticks and thorns. And he ate tamarisks and milkweed. And he ate prickles. He was most 'scruciating idle. And when anybody spoke to him he said "Humph!" Just "Humph!" and no more.

The Horse came to him on Monday morning. The Horse had a saddle on his back. And he had a bit in his mouth. He said, "Camel, O Camel, come out and trot like the rest of us." "Humph!" said the Camel. The Horse went away and told the Man.

The Dog came to him. The Dog had a stick in his mouth. He said, "Camel, O Camel, come and fetch and carry like the rest of us." "Humph!" said the Camel. The Dog went away and told the Man.

The Ox came to him. The Ox had the yoke on his neck. He said, "Camel, O Camel, come and plough like the rest of us." "Humph!" said the Camel. The Ox went away and told the Man.

At the end of the day the Man called the Horse and the Dog and the Ox. He said, "Three, O three, I'm very sorry for you (with the world so new-and-all). But that humph-thing in the desert can't work. Or he would have been here by now. So I am going to leave him alone. You must work double-time to make up for it."

There came along the Djinn in charge of all deserts. He was rolling in a cloud of dust. Djinn always travels that way. It is magic. He stopped to talk with the three. "Djinn of all deserts," said the Horse, "is it right for any one to be idle, with the world so new-and-all?"

"Certainly not," said the Djinn. "Well," said the Horse, "there's a thing in the middle of your Howling Desert. He is a howler himself. He has a long neck and long legs. He has not done a stroke of work since Monday morning. He will not trot."

"Whew!" said the Djinn, whistling. "That is my Camel, for all the gold in Arabia!" The Djinn rolled himself up in his dust-cloak. He went across the desert. He found the Camel most 'scruciatingly idle, looking at his own reflection in a pool of water.

"My long and bubbling friend," said the Djinn, "what's this I hear of your doing no work, with the world so new-and-all?"

"Humph!" said the Camel. The Djinn sat down, with his chin in his hand, and began to think a great magic. The Camel looked at his own reflection in the pool of water. "You've given the three extra work ever since Monday morning, all on account of your 'scruciating idleness," said the Djinn. And he went on thinking magics, with his chin in his hand.

"Humph!" said the Camel.

"I shouldn't say that again if I were you," said the Djinn. "You might say it once too often. Bubbles, I want you to work."

And the Camel said "Humph!" again. But no sooner had he said it than he saw his back, that he was so proud of, puffing up and puffing up into a great big lolloping humph.

"Do you see that?" said the Djinn. "That's your very own humph that you've brought upon your very own self by not working. Today is Thursday, and you've done no work since Monday, when the work began. Now you are going to work."

"How can I," said the Camel, "with this humph on my back?"

"That's made a-purpose," said the Djinn. "It is because you missed those three days. You will be able to work now for three days without eating. You can live on your humph. And don't you ever say I never did anything for you. Come out of the desert. Go to the three and behave. Humph yourself!'

Element Focus: Language Usage

Find several phrases that get repeated. How do the repeated phrases affect how you feel about the story?

Excerpt from

How the Camel Got His Hump

by Rudyard Kippling

In the beginning of years, when the world was so new and all, the animals were just beginning to work for Man. There was a Camel. He lived in the middle of a Howling Desert because he did not want to work. And besides, he was a howler himself. So he ate sticks and thorns and tamarisks and milkweed and prickles. He was most 'scruciating idle. And when anybody spoke to him, he said "Humph!" Just "Humph!" and no more.

Presently the Horse came to him on Monday morning, with a saddle on his back and a bit in his mouth. The Horse said, "Camel, O Camel, come out and trot like the rest of us." "Humph!" said the Camel. The Horse went away and told the Man.

Presently the Dog came to him, with a stick in his mouth. The Dog said, "Camel, O Camel, come and fetch and carry like the rest of us." "Humph!" said the Camel. The Dog went away and told the Man.

Presently the Ox came to him, with the yoke on his neck and said, "Camel, O Camel, come and plough like the rest of us." "Humph!" said the Camel. The Ox went away and told the Man.

At the end of the day, the Man called the Horse and the Dog and the Ox together. He said, "Three, O three, I'm very sorry for you (with the world so new-and-all). But that humph-thing in the desert can't work. Or he would have been here by now. So I am going to leave him alone. You must work double-time to make up for it."

Presently there came along the Djinn in charge of all deserts, rolling in a cloud of dust. Djinn always travels that way because it is magic. He stopped to palaver and pow-pow with the three. "Djinn of all deserts," said the Horse, "is it right for any one to be idle, with the world so new-and-all?"

"Certainly not," said the Djinn. "Well," said the Horse, "there's a thing in the middle of your Howling Desert (and he's a howler himself) with a long neck and long legs. He hasn't done a stroke of work since Monday morning. He won't trot.'

"Whew!" said the Djinn, whistling, "that's my Camel, for all the gold in Arabia!" The Djinn rolled himself up in his dust-cloak, and took a bearing across the desert. He found the Camel most 'scruciatingly idle, looking at his own reflection in a pool of water.

"My long and bubbling friend," said the Djinn, "what's this I hear of your doing no work, with the world so new-and-all?"

"Humph!" said the Camel. The Djinn sat down, with his chin in his hand, and began to think a Great Magic. The Camel looked at his own reflection in the pool of water. "You've given the Three extra work ever since Monday morning, all on account of your 'scruciating idleness," said the Djinn. And he went on thinking Magics, with his chin in his hand.

"Humph!" said the Camel.

"I shouldn't say that again if I were you," said the Djinn. "You might say it once too often. Bubbles, I want you to work."

And the Camel said "Humph!" again. But no sooner had he said it than he saw his back, that he was so proud of, puffing up and puffing up into a great big lolloping humph.

"Do you see that?" said the Djinn. "That's your very own humph that you've brought upon your very own self by not working. Today is Thursday, and you've done no work since Monday, when the work began. Now you are going to work."

"How can I," said the Camel, "with this humph on my back?"

"That's made a-purpose," said the Djinn, "all because you missed those three days. You will be able to work now for three days without eating, because you can live on your humph. And don't you ever say I never did anything for you. Come out of the desert and go to the three and behave. Humph yourself!"

Element Focus: Language Usage

Give at least three examples of phrases that Kippling chose to repeat throughout the story. What if he had not repeated these phrases? How would the story feel different?

Excerpt from

How the Camel Got His Hump

by Rudyard Kippling

In the beginning of years, when the world was so new and all, and the animals were just beginning to work for Man, there was a Camel, and he lived in the middle of a Howling Desert because he did not want to work; and besides, he was a howler himself. So he ate sticks and thorns and tamarisks and milkweed and prickles, most 'scruciating idle; and when anybody spoke to him he said "Humph!" Just "Humph!" and no more.

Presently the Horse came to him on Monday morning, with a saddle on his back and a bit in his mouth, and said, "Camel, O Camel, come out and trot like the rest of us." "Humph!" said the Camel; and the Horse went away and told the Man.

Presently the Dog came to him, with a stick in his mouth, and said, 'Camel, O Camel, come and fetch and carry like the rest of us." "Humph!" said the Camel; and the Dog went away and told the Man.

Presently the Ox came to him, with the yoke on his neck and said, "Camel, O Camel, come and plough like the rest of us." "Humph!" said the Camel; and the Ox went away and told the Man.

At the end of the day, the Man called the Horse and the Dog and the Ox together, and said, "Three, O three, I'm very sorry for you (with the world so new-and-all); but that humph-thing in the desert can't work, or he would have been here by now, so I am going to leave him alone, and you must work double-time to make up for it."

Presently there came along the Djinn in charge of all deserts, rolling in a cloud of dust (Djinn always travels that way because it is magic), and he stopped to palaver and pow-pow with the three. "Djinn of all deserts," said the Horse, "is it right for any one to be idle, with the world so new-and-all?"

"Certainly not," said the Djinn. "Well," said the Horse, 'there's a thing in the middle of your Howling Desert (and he's a howler himself) with a long neck and long legs, and he hasn't done a stroke of work since Monday morning. He won't trot.'

"Whew!" said the Djinn, whistling, "that's my Camel, for all the gold in Arabia!" The Djinn rolled himself up in his dust-cloak, and took a bearing across the desert, and found the Camel most 'scruciatingly idle, looking at his own reflection in a pool of water.

"My long and bubbling friend," said the Djinn, "what's this I hear of your doing no work, with the world so new-and-all?"

"Humph!" said the Camel. The Djinn sat down, with his chin in his hand, and began to think a Great Magic, while the Camel looked at his own reflection in the pool of water. "You've given the three extra work ever since Monday morning, all on account of your 'scruciating idleness," said the Djinn; and he went on thinking Magics, with his chin in his hand.

"Humph!" said the Camel.

"I shouldn't say that again if I were you," said the Djinn; "you might say it once too often. Bubbles, I want you to work."

And the Camel said "Humph!" again; but no sooner had he said it than he saw his back, that he was so proud of, puffing up and puffing up into a great big lolloping humph.

"Do you see that?" said the Djinn. "That's your very own humph that you've brought upon your very own self by not working. Today is Thursday, and you've done no work since Monday, when the work began. Now you are going to work."

"How can I," said the Camel, "with this humph on my back?"

"That's made a-purpose," said the Djinn, "all because you missed those three days. You will be able to work now for three days without eating, because you can live on your humph; and don't you ever say I never did anything for you. Come out of the desert and go to the three and behave. Humph yourself!"

Element Focus: Language Usage

Explain several reasons why Kippling might have chosen to repeat phrases throughout the story.

Excerpt from

How the Camel Got His Hump

by Rudyard Kippling

In the beginning of years, when the world was so new and all, and the animals were just beginning to work for Man, there was a Camel, and he lived in the middle of a Howling Desert because he did not want to work; and besides, he was a howler himself. So he ate sticks and thorns and tamarisks and milkweed and prickles, staying most 'scruciating idle, and when anybody spoke to him he said "Humph!" Simply "Humph!" and no more.

Presently the Horse came to him on Monday morning, with a saddle on his back and a bit in his mouth, and said, "Camel, O Camel, come out and trot like the rest of us." "Humph!" said the Camel, and the Horse went away and told the Man.

Presently the Dog came to him, with a stick in his mouth, and said, "Camel, O Camel, come and fetch and carry like the rest of us." "Humph!" said the Camel, and the Dog went away and told the Man.

Presently the Ox came to him, with the yoke on his neck and said, "Camel, O Camel, come and plough like the rest of us." "Humph!" said the Camel, and the Ox went away and told the Man.

As the day ended, the Man called the Horse and the Dog and the Ox together, and said, "Three, O three, I'm extremely sorry for you (with the world so new-and-all), but that humph-thing in the desert obviously can't work, or he would have been here by now, so I am going to leave him alone, and you must work double-time to make up for it."

Presently there came along the Djinn in charge of all deserts, rolling in a cloud of dust (Djinn always travels that way because it is magic), and he stopped to palaver and pow-pow with the Three. "Djinn of all deserts," inquired the Horse, "is it right for any one to be idle, with the world so new-and-all?"

"Certainly not," declared the Djinn. "Well," said the Horse, "there's a thing in the middle of your Howling Desert (and he's a howler himself) with a long neck and long legs, and he hasn't done a stroke of work since Monday morning. He refuses to trot."

"Whew!" said the Djinn, whistling, "that's my Camel, for all the gold in Arabia!" The Djinn rolled himself up in his dust-cloak, and took a bearing across the desert, and found the Camel most 'scruciatingly idle, admiring his own reflection in a pool of water.

"My long and bubbling friend," said the Djinn, "what's this I have been told of your doing no work, with the world so new-and-all?"

"Humph!" said the Camel. The Djinn sat down, with his chin in his hand, and began to think a Great Magic, while the Camel looked at his own reflection in the pool of water. "You've given the three extra work ever since Monday morning, all on account of your 'scruciating idleness," said the Djinn, and he went on conjuring Magics, with his chin in his hand.

"Humph!" said the Camel.

"I shouldn't say that again if I were you," said the Djinn; "you might say it once too often. Bubbles, I want you to work."

And the Camel said "Humph!" again; but no sooner had he said it than he saw his back, that he was so proud of, puffing up and puffing up into a great big lolloping humph.

"Do you see that?" said the Djinn. "That's your very own humph that you've brought upon your very own self by not working. Today is Thursday, and you've done no work since Monday, when the work began. Now you are going to work."

"How can I," said the Camel, "with this humph on my back?"

"That's made a-purpose," said the Djinn, "all because you missed those three days. You will be able to work now for three days without eating, because you can live on your humph; and don't you ever say I never did anything for you. Come out of the desert and go to the three and behave. Humph yourself!"

Element Focus: Language Usage

In what ways did the inclusion of repeated phrases increase or decrease the humor of the story?

Excerpt from

My Father's Dragon

by Ruth Stiles Gannett

The tigers walked around him. They made a big circle. Every second they looked hungrier. And then they sat down. They began to talk. "I bet you thought we didn't know you were here! You are in our jungle without our say so! That is trespassing!"

Then the next tiger spoke. "I bet you will say you didn't know it was our jungle!"

"Not one explorer has ever left this island alive!" said the third tiger. My father thought of the cat. So he knew this wasn't true. But he had too much sense to say so. One doesn't argue with a hungry tiger.

The tigers went on talking. Each took a turn. "You're our first little boy. I'm curious. I wonder if you are extra tender."

"Maybe you think we have regular meal-times. But we do not. We eat whenever we feel hungry," said the fifth tiger.

"And we are very hungry right now. In fact, I can hardly wait," said the sixth.

"I *can't* wait!" said the seventh tiger.

Then all the tigers spoke together. They roared, "Let us start right now!" And they moved in closer. My father looked. He saw those seven hungry tigers. And he had an idea. He opened his knapsack. He took out the chewing gum. The cat had told him that tigers really like gum. And it was very rare on the island. So he threw a piece to each one. But they only growled. "We do like gum. But we are sure we would like you even better!" They moved closer. They were so close that he could feel them breathing on his face.

"But this is very special gum," said my father. "Keep chewing it long enough, and it will turn green. Then you can plant it. And it will grow more! The sooner you start the sooner you will have more."

The tigers said, "Why, you don't say! Isn't that fine!" Each one wanted to be the first to plant the gum. So they all unwrapped their pieces. They began chewing. They chewed as hard as they could. Every once in a while one tiger would look into another's mouth. He would say, "Nope, it's not done yet." Soon, they were all busy looking into each other's mouths. They wanted to make sure that no one was getting ahead. They forgot all about my father!

My father walked back and forth. He was trying to think. He needed a way to cross the river. He found a high flagpole. It had a rope going over to the other side. He was about to start up the pole. The monkeys made a lot of noise. But he heard a loud splash behind him. He looked all around in the water. But it was dusk now. He could not see anything.

"It's me, Crocodile," said a voice to the left. "The water's lovely! I have such a craving for something sweet. Won't you come in for a swim?" A pale moon came out from behind the clouds. My father could see where the voice was coming from. The crocodile's head was just peeping out of the water.

"Oh, no thank you," said my father. "I never swim after sundown. But I do have something sweet to offer you. Perhaps you'd like a lollipop! And, perhaps you have friends who would like lollipops, too?"

"Lollipops!" said the crocodile. "Why, that is a treat! How about it, boys?" A whole chorus of voices shouted, "Hurrah! Lollipops!" My father counted as many as seventeen crocodiles with their heads just peeping out of the water.

"That's fine," said my father as he got out the two dozen pink lollipops and the rubber bands. "I'll stick one here in the bank. Lollipops last longer if you keep them out of the water, you know. Now, one of you can have this one."

The crocodile who had first spoken swam up and tasted it. "Delicious, mighty delicious!" he said. "Now if you don't mind," said my father, "I'll just walk along your back. Then I will fasten another lollipop. I will put it on the tip of your tail with a rubber band. You don't mind, do you?"

Element Focus: Language Usage

Describe the tigers and the crocodiles.
In what ways are they like people?

My Father's Dragon

by Ruth Gannett

The tigers walked around him in a big circle. They were looking hungrier all the time. And then they sat down and began to talk. "I suppose you thought we didn't know you were trespassing in our jungle!"

Then the next tiger spoke. "I suppose you're going to say you didn't know it was our jungle!"

"Did you know that not one explorer has ever left this island alive?" said the third tiger. My father thought of the cat and knew this wasn't true. But of course he had too much sense to say so. One doesn't contradict a hungry tiger.

The tigers went on talking. Each took a turn. "You're our first little boy, you know. I'm curious. I wonder if you are especially tender."

"Maybe you think we have regular meal-times. But we don't. We just eat whenever we're feeling hungry," said the fifth tiger.

"And we're very hungry right now. In fact, I can hardly wait," said the sixth.

"I *can't* wait!" said the seventh tiger.

And then all the tigers spoke together. They said in a loud roar, "Let's begin right now!" And they moved in closer. My father looked at those seven hungry tigers. Then he had an idea. He quickly opened his knapsack. He took out the chewing gum. The cat had told him that tigers were especially fond of chewing gum. And it was very rare on the island. So he threw them each a piece. But they only growled, "As fond as we are of chewing gum, we're sure we'd like you even better!" They moved so close that he could feel them breathing on his face.

"But this is very special chewing gum," said my father. "If you keep on chewing it long enough, it will turn green. Then if you plant it, it will grow more chewing gum! The sooner you start chewing, the sooner you'll have more."

The tigers said, "Why, you don't say! Isn't that fine!" Each one wanted to be the first to plant the chewing gum. So they all unwrapped their pieces and began chewing as hard as they could. Every once in a while one tiger would look into another's mouth and say, "Nope, it's not done yet," Finally, they were all so busy looking into each other's mouths to make sure that no one was getting ahead that they forgot all about my father.

My father walked back and forth along the bank. He was trying to think of some way to cross the river. He found a high flagpole with a rope going over to the other side. He was about to start up the pole. But despite all the noise the monkeys were making, he heard a loud splash behind him. He looked all around in the water. But it was dusk now. He couldn't see anything there.

"It's me, Crocodile," said a voice to the left. "The water's lovely! I have such a craving for something sweet. Won't you come in for a swim?" A pale moon came out from behind the clouds. My father could see where the voice was coming from. The crocodile's head was just peeping out of the water.

"Oh, no thank you," said my father. "I never swim after sundown. But I do have something sweet to offer you. Perhaps you'd like a lollipop! And, perhaps you have friends who would like lollipops, too?"

"Lollipops!" said the crocodile. "Why, that is a treat! How about it, boys?" A whole chorus of voices shouted, "Hurrah! Lollipops!" My father counted as many as seventeen crocodiles with their heads just peeping out of the water.

"That's fine," said my father as he got out the two dozen pink lollipops and the rubber bands. "I'll stick one here in the bank. Lollipops last longer if you keep them out of the water, you know. Now, one of you can have this one."

The crocodile who had first spoken swam up and tasted it. "Delicious, mighty delicious!" he said. "Now if you don't mind," said my father, "I'll just walk along your back. Then I will fasten another lollipop to the tip of your tail with a rubber band. You don't mind, do you?"

Element Focus: Language Usage

In what ways are the tigers and crocodiles personified in the text?

Excerpt from

My Father's Dragon

by Ruth Stiles Gannett

The tigers walked around him in a big circle, looking hungrier all the time, and then they sat down and began to talk. "I suppose you thought we didn't know you were trespassing in our jungle!"

Then the next tiger spoke. "I suppose you're going to say you didn't know it was our jungle!"

"Did you know that not one explorer has ever left this island alive?" said the third tiger. My father thought of the cat and knew this wasn't true. But of course he had too much sense to say so. One doesn't contradict a hungry tiger.

The tigers went on talking in turn. "You're our first little boy, you know. I'm curious to know if you're especially tender."

"Maybe you think we have regular meal-times, but we don't. We just eat whenever we're feeling hungry," said the fifth tiger.

"And we're very hungry right now. In fact, I can hardly wait," said the sixth.

"I *can't* wait!" said the seventh tiger.

And then all the tigers said together in a loud roar, "Let's begin right now!" and they moved in closer. My father looked at those seven hungry tigers, and then he had an idea. He quickly opened his knapsack and took out the chewing gum. The cat had told him that tigers were especially fond of chewing gum, which was very scarce on the island. So he threw them each a piece but they only growled, "As fond as we are of chewing gum, we're sure we'd like you even better!" and they moved so close that he could feel them breathing on his face.

"But this is very special chewing gum," said my father. "If you keep on chewing it long enough it will turn green, and then if you plant it, it will grow more chewing gum, and the sooner you start chewing the sooner you'll have more."

The tigers said, "Why, you don't say! Isn't that fine!" And as each one wanted to be the first to plant the chewing gum, they all unwrapped their pieces and began chewing as hard as they could. Every once in a while one tiger would look into another's mouth and say, "Nope, it's not done yet," until finally they were all so busy looking into each other's mouths to make sure that no one was getting ahead that they forgot all about my father.

My father walked back and forth along the bank trying to think of some way to cross the river. He found a high flagpole with a rope going over to the other side. He was about to start up the pole when, despite all the noise the monkeys were making, he heard a loud splash behind him. He looked all around in the water but it was dusk now, and he couldn't see anything there.

"It's me, Crocodile," said a voice to the left. "The water's lovely, and I have such a craving for something sweet. Won't you come in for a swim?" A pale moon came out from behind the clouds and my father could see where the voice was coming from. The crocodile's head was just peeping out of the water.

"Oh, no thank you," said my father. "I never swim after sundown, but I do have something sweet to offer you. Perhaps you'd like a lollipop, and perhaps you have friends who would like lollipops, too?"

"Lollipops!" said the crocodile. "Why, that is a treat! How about it, boys?" A whole chorus of voices shouted, "Hurrah! Lollipops!" and my father counted as many as seventeen crocodiles with their heads just peeping out of the water.

"That's fine," said my father as he got out the two dozen pink lollipops and the rubber bands. "I'll stick one here in the bank. Lollipops last longer if you keep them out of the water, you know. Now, one of you can have this one."

The crocodile who had first spoken swam up and tasted it. "Delicious, mighty delicious!" he said. "Now if you don't mind," said my father, "I'll just walk along your back and fasten another lollipop to the tip of your tail with a rubber band. You don't mind, do you?"

Element Focus: Language Usage

What are some examples of personification in the text.

My Father's Dragon

by Ruth Stiles Gannett

The tigers prowled around him in a big circle, appearing to grow constantly hungrier, and then they abruptly crouched down and began to speak. "I suppose you were under the impression that we were unaware that you were trespassing in our jungle!"

Then the next tiger spoke. "I suppose you're going to deny that you knew it was our jungle!"

"Were you aware that not a single explorer has ever left this island alive?" demanded the third tiger. My father thought of the cat and knew this wasn't true, but of course he had too much sense to say so. One simply doesn't contradict a hungry tiger.

The tigers continued speaking in turn. "You're our first little boy, you know, so I'm curious to know if you're especially tender."

"Maybe you think we have regular meal-times, but we don't. We simplify matters by dining whenever we're feeling hungry," said the fifth tiger.

"And I should probably mention that we are extremely hungry right now. In fact, I can hardly wait to take my first bite," confessed the sixth.

"I *can't* wait!" declared the seventh tiger emphatically.

And then all the tigers said together in a loud roar, "Let's begin right now!" and they moved in closer. My father peered at those seven hungry tigers, and then he had an idea. He swiftly opened his knapsack and retrieved the chewing gum he had stashed there. The cat had informed him that tigers were especially fond of chewing gum, which was very scarce on the island. So he distributed a piece to each of them, but they only growled, "As fond as we are of chewing gum, we're sure we'd like you even better!" and they advanced so close that he could feel them breathing on his face.

"But this is very special chewing gum," said my father. "If you keep on chewing it long enough, it will turn green, and then, if you plant it, it will grow more chewing gum. The sooner you start chewing, the sooner you'll have more."

The tigers said, "Why, you don't say! Isn't that fine!" And as each one wanted to be the first to plant the chewing gum, they all unwrapped their pieces and began chewing as hard as they could. Every once in a while, one tiger would look into another's mouth and say, "Nope, it's not done yet," until finally they were all so busy looking into each other's mouths to make sure that no one was getting ahead that they forgot all about my father.

My father paced thoughtfully along the bank trying to think of some convenient way to cross the river. He found a high flagpole with a rope going over to the other side and was about to start up the pole when, despite all the noise the monkeys were making, he heard a loud splash behind him. He looked all around in the water but it was dusk now, and he couldn't distinguish anything identifiable.

"It's me, Crocodile," said a voice to the left. "The water's lovely, and I have such a craving for something sweet, so won't you come in for a swim?" A pale moon came out from behind the clouds and my father could just determine where the voice was coming from. The crocodile's head was barely peeping out of the water.

"Oh, no thank you," said my father. "I never swim after sundown, but I do have something sweet to offer you. Perhaps you'd like a lollipop, and perhaps you have friends who would enjoy lollipops, too?"

"Lollipops!" cried the crocodile happily. "Why, that is a treat! How about it, boys?" A whole chorus of voices shouted, "Hurrah! Lollipops!" and my father counted as many as seventeen crocodiles with their heads just peeping out of the water.

"That's fine," said my father as he got out the two dozen pink lollipops and the rubber bands. "I'll stick one here in the bank since lollipops last longer if you keep them out of the water, you know. Now, one of you can have this one."

The crocodile who had first spoken swam up and tasted it. "Delicious, mighty delicious!" he declared. "Now if you don't mind," said my father politely, "I'll just walk along your back and fasten another lollipop to the tip of your tail with a rubber band. You don't mind, do you?"

Element Focus: Language Usage

Give several examples of ways that personification is used to heighten the humor of the story.

Excerpt from

The Wonderful Wizard of Oz

by L. Frank Baum

The next morning the Scarecrow said:

"Congratulate me. I am going to Oz to get my brains at last. When I return I shall be like other men."

"I have always liked you as you were," said Dorothy simply.

"It is kind of you to like a Scarecrow," he said. "But you will think more of me when you hear the great thoughts of my new brain." Then he said a cheerful good-bye. And he went to the Throne Room. There he rapped on the door.

"Come in," said Oz. The Scarecrow went in. He found the little man sitting down by the window. He was in deep thought.

"I have come for my brains," said the Scarecrow. He felt a little uneasy.

"Oh, yes. Sit down in that chair, please," said Oz. "I am sorry. I must take your head off. I have to so I can put your brains in their right place."

"That is fine," said the Scarecrow. "You can take my head off. Just please make sure it is a better one when you put it back on."

So the Wizard unfastened his head. He emptied out the straw. Then he went to the back room. He took up a measure of bran. This he mixed with many pins and needles. He shook them together thoroughly. Then he filled the top of the Scarecrow's head with the mixture. He stuffed the rest of the space with straw.

Then he put the Scarecrow's head on his body again. He said to him, "Now you will be a great man. I have given you a lot of bran-new brains."

The Scarecrow was pleased. And he was proud. This was the fulfillment of his greatest wish. He thanked Oz warmly. Then he went back to his friends.

Dorothy looked at him curiously. His head was bulged out at the top with brains.

"How do you feel?" she asked.

"I feel truly wise," he answered. "When I get used to my brains I will know everything."

"Why are those needles and pins sticking out of your head?" asked the Tin Woodman.

"That is proof that he is sharp," said the Lion. The Lion now walked to the Throne Room. He knocked at the door. "Come in," said Oz.

"I have come for my courage," said the Lion. He went in.

"Very well," said the little man. "I will get it for you." He went to a cupboard. Reaching up to a high shelf, he took down a square green bottle. He poured the contents into a green-gold dish. It was beautifully carved. He placed this before the Cowardly Lion. The lion sniffed at it as if he did not like it. The Wizard said: "Drink."

"What is it?" asked the Lion.

"Well," answered Oz, "if it were inside of you, it would be courage. You know, of course, that courage is always inside one; so that this really cannot be called courage until you have swallowed it. Therefore, I advise you to drink it as soon as possible."

The Lion hesitated no longer. He drank till the dish was empty. "How do you feel now?" asked Oz.

"Full of courage," said the Lion. Then he went joyfully back to his friends to tell them of his good fortune.

Element Focus: Language Usage

Sometimes humor comes from playing with words. One word can have more than one meaning. What does the Lion mean when he says that the pins and needles show that the Scarecrow is *sharp*?

Excerpt from
The Wonderful Wizard of Oz

by L. Frank Baum

Next morning the Scarecrow said to his friends:

"Congratulate me. I am going to Oz to get my brains at last. When I return I shall be as other men are."

"I have always liked you as you were," said Dorothy simply.

"It is kind of you to like a Scarecrow," he replied. "But you will think more of me when you hear the great thoughts my new brain is going to turn out." Then he said good-bye to them all in a cheerful voice. And he went to the Throne Room. There he rapped upon the door.

"Come in," said Oz. The Scarecrow went in. He found the little man sitting down by the window, engaged in deep thought.

"I have come for my brains," said the Scarecrow. He felt a little uneasy.

"Oh, yes. Sit down in that chair, please," replied Oz. "You must excuse me for taking your head off. But I shall have to do it in order to put your brains in their proper place."

"That's all right," said the Scarecrow. "You are quite welcome to take my head off, as long as it will be a better one when you put it on again."

So the Wizard unfastened his head and emptied out the straw. Then he entered the back room. He took up a measure of bran, which he mixed with a great many pins and needles. He shook them together thoroughly. Then he filled the top of the Scarecrow's head with the mixture. He stuffed the rest of the space with straw to hold it in place.

When he had fastened the Scarecrow's head on his body again he said to him, "Now you will be a great man. I have given you a lot of bran-new brains."

The Scarecrow was both pleased and proud at the fulfillment of his greatest wish. Having thanked Oz warmly, he went back to his friends.

Dorothy looked at him curiously. His head was quite bulged out at the top with brains.

"How do you feel?" she asked.

"I feel wise indeed," he answered earnestly. "When I get used to my brains I shall know everything."

"Why are those needles and pins sticking out of your head?" asked the Tin Woodman.

"That is proof that he is sharp," said the Lion. The Lion now walked to the Throne Room. He knocked at the door. "Come in," said Oz.

"I have come for my courage," announced the Lion. He entered the room.

"Very well," answered the little man. "I will get it for you." He went to a cupboard, and reaching up to a high shelf, took down a square green bottle. He poured the contents into a green-gold dish, beautifully carved. He placed this before the Cowardly Lion who sniffed at it as if he did not like it. The Wizard said: "Drink."

"What is it?" asked the Lion.

"Well," answered Oz, "if it were inside of you, it would be courage. You know, of course, that courage is always inside one; so that this really cannot be called courage until you have swallowed it. Therefore I advise you to drink it as soon as possible."

The Lion hesitated no longer, but drank till the dish was empty. "How do you feel now?" asked Oz.

"Full of courage," replied the Lion, who went joyfully back to his friends to tell them of his good fortune.

Element Focus: Language Usage

Sometimes humor comes from playing with words.
What does Oz mean when he says that
the scarecrow has *bran-new brains*?

The Wonderful Wizard of Oz

by L. Frank Baum

Next morning the Scarecrow said to his friends: "Congratulate me. I am going to Oz to get my brains at last. When I return I shall be as other men are."

"I have always liked you as you were," said Dorothy simply.

"It is kind of you to like a Scarecrow," he replied. "But surely you will think more of me when you hear the splendid thoughts my new brain is going to turn out." Then he said good-bye to them all in a cheerful voice and went to the Throne Room, where he rapped upon the door.

"Come in," said Oz. The Scarecrow went in and found the little man sitting down by the window, engaged in deep thought.

"I have come for my brains," remarked the Scarecrow, a little uneasily.

"Oh, yes; sit down in that chair, please," replied Oz. "You must excuse me for taking your head off, but I shall have to do it in order to put your brains in their proper place."

"That's all right," said the Scarecrow. "You are quite welcome to take my head off, as long as it will be a better one when you put it on again."

So the Wizard unfastened his head and emptied out the straw. Then he entered the back room and took up a measure of bran, which he mixed with a great many pins and needles. Having shaken them together thoroughly, he filled the top of the Scarecrow's head with the mixture and stuffed the rest of the space with straw, to hold it in place.

When he had fastened the Scarecrow's head on his body again he said to him, "Hereafter you will be a great man, for I have given you a lot of bran-new brains."

The Scarecrow was both pleased and proud at the fulfillment of his greatest wish, and having thanked Oz warmly he went back to his friends.

Dorothy looked at him curiously. His head was quite bulged out at the top with brains.

"How do you feel?" she asked.

"I feel wise indeed," he answered earnestly. "When I get used to my brains I shall know everything."

"Why are those needles and pins sticking out of your head?" asked the Tin Woodman.

"That is proof that he is sharp," remarked the Lion. The Lion now walked to the Throne Room and knocked at the door. "Come in," said Oz.

"I have come for my courage," announced the Lion, entering the room.

"Very well," answered the little man; "I will get it for you." He went to a cupboard and reaching up to a high shelf took down a square green bottle, the contents of which he poured into a green-gold dish, beautifully carved. Placing this before the Cowardly Lion, who sniffed at it as if he did not like it, the Wizard said: "Drink."

"What is it?" asked the Lion.

"Well," answered Oz, "if it were inside of you, it would be courage. You know, of course, that courage is always inside one; so that this really cannot be called courage until you have swallowed it. Therefore I advise you to drink it as soon as possible."

The Lion hesitated no longer, but drank till the dish was empty. "How do you feel now?" asked Oz.

"Full of courage," replied the Lion, who went joyfully back to his friends to tell them of his good fortune.

Element Focus: Language Usage

Sometimes humor comes from playing with words. In what ways did the author play with words in this passage?

Excerpt from
The Wonderful Wizard of Oz

by L. Frank Baum

Next morning the Scarecrow said to his friends: "Congratulate me because I am going to Oz to finally get my brains. When I return I shall be just as other men are."

"I have always liked you as you were," said Dorothy simply.

"It is kind of you to like a Scarecrow," he replied. "But surely you will think more of me when you hear the splendid thoughts my new brain is going to turn out." Then he said good-bye to them all in a cheerful voice and went to the Throne Room, where he rapped upon the door.

"Come in," said Oz, so the Scarecrow went in and found the little man sitting down by the window, engaged in deep thought.

"I have come for my brains," remarked the Scarecrow, a little uneasily.

"Oh, yes, of course, sit down in that chair, please," replied Oz. "You must excuse me for removing your head, but it is a necessary part of the process in order to put your brains in their proper place."

"That's all right," said the Scarecrow. "You are quite welcome to take my head off, as long as it will be a better one when you reattach it in its proper position."

So the Wizard unfastened his head and emptied out the straw. Then he entered the back room and took up a measure of bran, which he mixed with a great many pins and needles. Having shaken them together thoroughly, he filled the top of the Scarecrow's head with the mixture and stuffed the rest of the space with straw, to hold it all in place. When he had fastened the Scarecrow's head firmly on his body again he said to him, "Hereafter you will be a great man, for I have given you a lot of bran-new brains."

The Scarecrow was both pleased and proud at the fulfillment of his greatest wish, and having thanked Oz warmly he went back to his friends.

Dorothy looked at him curiously, since his head was quite bulged out at the top with brains.

"How do you feel?" she asked carefully.

"I feel wise indeed," he answered earnestly. "When I become accustomed to my brains I shall know everything."

"Why are those needles and pins sticking out of your head?" inquired the Tin Woodman curiously.

"That is proof that he is sharp," remarked the Lion. The Lion now walked to the Throne Room and knocked at the door. "Enter, please," said Oz.

"I have come for my courage," announced the Lion in a clear voice, entering the room.

"Very well," answered the little man, "I will get it for you." He went to a cupboard, and reaching up to a high shelf, took down a square green bottle, the contents of which he poured into a green-gold dish, beautifully carved. Placing this before the Cowardly Lion, who sniffed at it as if he did not like it, the Wizard directed: "Drink it, if you please."

"What is it?" asked the Lion, a bit sheepishly.

"Well," answered Oz, "if it were inside of you, it would be courage. You know, of course, that courage is always inside one, so that this really cannot be called courage until you have swallowed it. Therefore I advise you to drink it as soon as possible."

The Lion hesitated no longer, but drank till the dish was empty. "How do you feel now?" asked Oz.

"Full of courage," replied the Lion, who went joyfully back to his friends to tell them of his good fortune.

Element Focus: Language Usage

Describe the ways that the author played with language to create humor in this passage.

References Cited

Bean, Thomas. 2000. Reading in the Content Areas: Social Constructivist Dimensions. In *Handbook of Reading Research, vol. 3*, eds. M. Kamil, P. Mosenthal, P. D. Pearson, and R. Barr. Mahwah, NJ: Lawrence Erlbaum.

Bromley, Karen. 2004. Rethinking Vocabulary Instruction. *The Language and Literacy Spectrum* 14:3–12.

Melville, Herman. 1851. *Moby Dick*. New York: Harper.

Nagy, William, and Richard C. Anderson. 1984. How Many Words Are There in Printed School English? *Reading Research Quarterly* 19 (3): 304–330.

National Governors Association Center for Best Practices and Council of Chief State School Officers. 2010. Common Core Standards. http://www.corestandards.org/the-standards.

Oatley, Keith. 2009. Changing Our Minds. *Greater Good: The Science of a Meaningful Life*, Winter. http://greatergood.berkeley.edu/article/item/chaning_our_minds.

Pinnell, Gay Su. 1988. Success of Children At Risk in a Program that Combines Writing and Reading. *Technical Report No.* 417 (January). Reading and Writing Connections.

Richek, Margaret. 2005. Words Are Wonderful: Interactive, Time-Efficient Strategies to Teach Meaning Vocabulary. *The Reading Teacher* 58 (5): 414–423.

Riordan, Rick. 2005. *The Lightning Thief*. London: Puffin Books.

Sachar, Louis. 2000. *Holes*. New York, NY: Dell Yearling.

Snicket, Lemony. 1999. *A Series of Unfortunate Events*. New York: HarperCollins.

Tomlinson, Carol Ann and Marcia. B. Imbeau. 2010. *Leading and Managing a Differentiated Classroom*. Alexandria, VA: Association for Supervision and Curriculum Development.

Zunshine, Lisa. 2006. *Why We Read Fiction: Theory of Mind and the Novel*. Columbus, OH: The Ohio State University Press.

Contents of the Digital Resource CD

Passage	Filename	Pages
The Adventures of Pinocchio	pinocchio.pdf pinocchio.doc	31–38
Mother Goose in Prose	prose.pdf prose.doc	39–46
Denslow's Three Bears	denslow.pdf denslow.doc	47–54
Alice's Adventures in Wonderland	alicewonder.pdf alicewonder.doc	55–62
Anne of Green Gables	annegreen.pdf annegreen.doc	63–70
The Magic Fishbone: A Holiday Romance from the Pen of Miss Alice Rainbird	magicfishbone.pdf magicfishbone.doc	71–78
The Book of Nature Myths: Why the Bear Has a Short Tail	bookmyths.pdf bookmyths.doc	79–86
The Bremen Town Musicians	brementown.pdf brementown.doc	87–94
Clever Else	cleverelse.pdf cleverelse.doc	95–102
The Story of Doctor Dolittle	doctordolittle.pdf doctordolittle.doc	103–110
Tales from Shakespeare	shakespeare.pdf shakespeare.doc	111–118
The Celebrated Jumping Frog of Calaveras County	jumpingfrog.pdf jumpingfrog.doc	119–126
How the Camel Got His Hump	camelhump.pdf camelhump.doc	127–134
My Father's Dragon	fathersdragon.pdf fathersdragon.doc	135–142
The Wonderful Wizard of Oz	wizardoz.pdf wizardoz.doc	143–150